Why Is There Salt in the Sea?

Brigitte Schwaiger

hy Is There Salt in the Sea?

Wie kommt das Salz ins Meer

Translated and with an afterword by Sieglinde Lug

University of Nebraska Press

Lincoln and London

The paper in this book meets the minimum require-
ments of American National Standard
for Information Sciences—Permanence of Paper
for Printed Library Materials, ANSI Z39.48–1984.

Library of Congress Cataloging-in-Publication Data
Schwaiger, Brigitte, 1949–
[Wie kommt das Salz ins Meer? English]
Why is there salt in the sea? - Wie kommt das Salz
ins Meer / by Brigitte Schwaiger; translated and
with an afterword by Sieglinde Lug.
p. cm. — (European women writers series)
Translation of: Wie kommt das Salz ins Meer?
ISBN 0-8032-4174-7 (alk. paper)
I. Title. II. Title: Wie kommt das Salz ins Meer?
III. Series.   PT2680.W26W513 1988   833′.914—dc19
87-21934

CONTENTS

I want to thank
Jeannine Blackwell,
Leland H. Chambers,
Tricia England,
and Marion Faber
for their valuable suggestions
to improve this translation.
SIEGLINDE LUG

Why Is There Salt in the Sea?

"That's it, quite right!
Relaxation!
That is the deeper meaning.
They are made for relaxation.
That is why I am against the
so-called interesting females.
Women should not be interesting
but pleasant."

ARTHUR SCHNITZLER, *Playing with Love*

Respectable, in front of the mirror in my parents' bedroom, respectable, that's the most important thing. Grandmother says it emphatically. The simple formula that has it all: consolation and reassurance when she says it: respectable. A zipper is stuck. It is hot, a window should be opened, stuffy air. Mother squeezes herself into her dress. The fabric has gotten caught in the zipper. Always that rag, says Father. That's not a rag, says Grandmother, that's good material. She rubs the seam between her fingers. Why always, asks Mother. She wore the dress only once, for Grandfather's funeral. It's elegant, says Grandmother. Father is getting impatient. He has been ready for an hour, was at the barber's yesterday to have his neck shaved. Black suit, white handkerchief, gray hat. Can I go like this, asks Grandmother. Yes, just go, go, who will see you anyway, no one looks at you, you're old, of course you can go like that, besides, you don't listen to anyone anyhow. Your fur cap sits much too low on your face again. You look like a Russian peasant woman. Yes, you can easily go like that, says Father. Mother's zipper is finally closed. She dabs off the small beads of sweat that have collected under her brows, then she puts on lipstick, even now she can be proud of that mouth. Polishes her purse quickly. The leather must shine. Father wants to know how long Mother has had this purse. For years, she says. Grandmother nods. I do not recognize that purse, Father declares. An elegant purse, says Grandmother, it goes with the shoes, and that's the most important thing. Mother smoothes out her gloves. She asks if she should wear one glove on the left hand and carry the right one loosely in her right hand. Your hand will freeze off, Grandmother warns. Hurry up, says Father.

And her? What is the matter with her? Why are you lying on the bed? Aren't you feeling well? Suddenly, three faces above me. You're crumpling your dress! Put on your shoes! Take your coat! Which coat? Yours, of course! That beautiful coat, says Grandmother, that's right, we needn't be ashamed of ourselves. I'll clean up a little, says Mother, so much stuff lying around, let me straighten up the room. No, Father is in a hurry. See, now your beautiful dress is crumpled. Why did you have to lie on the bed! Let me look at you! Why didn't you go to the beauty shop? Nervous, says Grandmother, if I think back! Don't think back, says Father, why don't you button your jacket instead. If I think back, says Grandmother, my God! She looks like a corpse! The child eats too little and smokes too much. Every day that black coffee on her empty stomach! Please don't use your cologne today, says Mother, and slips a little bottle into her hand. Of course they are going to sit next to each other and Grandmother's cologne does not agree with Mother. I always use my cologne! Grandmother says she's used to it. Anyway, she has to be careful with her money. Who says you have to watch your money, you get enough every month, Father shouts. I have to think of the future, says Grandmother. Come on now, says Father, or have you reconsidered?

What if I have reconsidered? What if we call and leave a message that we won't be coming? Maybe sometime, later, but not today. I did reconsider, I don't want to, because I never really wanted to, because you all outwitted me. Because you said: only a formality. And now you are all excited, take it so seriously, are all against me. Don't worry, my child, you said, it's only a tradition.

Father runs down the stairs whistling, Mother and Grandmother have taken each other's arm and follow slowly, since the old woman can't move fast anymore because of her knees, she has had to go up and down the stairs sideways ever since she got bursitis on an excursion to a Sicilian volcano, she brought home a whole box of lava bits, and her knees. They took handkerchiefs, just in case. They take handkerchiefs to the movies too, because they go only to sad movies so they can get their money's worth. Just like real life, says Grandmother. Next to our TV set there is always a box of gauze from Father's office. When there is news about an airplane crash, Mother cries. Also at news from the Sahel area or India, especially when they show pictures, and at old movies with O. W. Fischer and Ruth Leuwerik,[1] and at earthquakes. Ever since Kleenex they can cry more abundantly on all occasions.

All four doors are open, Father is standing next to the

1. An Austrian actor (b. 1915) and a German actress (b. 1926) who became famous in the fifties. Many of their films were sentimental love stories reminiscent of Hollywood melodrama.

5

car. Why are you pushing? The doors are all open! Oh leave us alone, says Mother. Just let us get in the way we want to, says Grandmother. She should sit in front. Who? You? Or shall I sit next to Father, says Mother. Quiet, Father requests, I'm driving now! I am getting sick of it. Always fighting, says Grandmother, I like that! Really, it's enough to drive you to despair, Mother whispers. Quiet, says Father, and put on your seat belts. Watch your dress, says Grandmother. Though she never does! She's not a lady! A lady would never sit like she does.

Dearest Rolf, I said, I don't want to go through with this. He brushed it aside with his hand. It's nothing but a fear of cold water. Jump in! I said I had suddenly lost courage. Then he came up with more words and built a wall without windows. After all, everything was settled. We would look foolish. I should have more faith in him, he said, like I used to. One day we would laugh about this together. You don't understand me, I said. How can you expect anyone to understand you, if you don't understand yourself? Those who are truly free, he said, don't feel restricted by formalities. We are not tramps, we are not gypsies, he said. Professionally and socially, I cannot afford to give in to your every whim. Say no, I will accept it. Yes or no? If you say no, I'll draw the appropriate conclusions, but as you know: I'm in the habit of persisting in what I have resolved to do.

Yes, I know. After the first semester at the Technical University, Rolf realized that medicine actually interested him more. However: what you have started you have to see through to the end. When I confessed that I had started writing something again he consoled me with embraces. I was nothing, but I was worth a lot to him. I couldn't do anything, but I could do a lot for him. He said: You're the only woman who doesn't bore me. I don't know what I would have done without Rolf. You don't need to know, he said, after all, you have me. We love each other. Is that nothing? What would he do with a wife who has no ambition? That's easy: I have enough ambition for both of us. That was true. On a gloomy Tuesday Rolf's doctoral graduation was celebrated in the auditorium of the university. He invited friends to the ceremony. I typed the addresses on the envelopes. At least you could have learned how to type, Rolf said. I came alone that day because I had to think about all that and also about the typing. Rolf went on ahead and asked me to be on time. Today I want to do everything right, starting today, I thought on that lightless Tuesday, you get ahead only with ambition, I reminded myself. I had always admired the girls at the university whose skirts got baggy from sitting and cramming, the unkempt ones who didn't have time for trifles.

On the bus that took me toward Rolf's goal, the people looked very serious. So did the driver. An old woman asked him if this was the right bus. The driver nodded. He started the engine in the knowledge that it was his duty to drive all passengers to today's doctoral graduation. He had sacrificed himself, had denied himself a college education to drive these people to the university. He let me come along because I had a ticket. But there was something like reproach in his eyes: you had a chance, but you did not make anything of your chance! The old woman who had asked him if that was the bus to the university pulled a handwritten letter from her purse. She unfolded it and read. Her nephew probably told her he would receive his doctorate today at eleven. Or perhaps it was her grandson. Or just a student who had lived in one of her empty rooms and had remembered the landlady and invited her. Next to the old woman there was a young teacher. I saw immediately that the blonde woman was a teacher. The old woman asked the teacher if you have to show the invitation when you enter the auditorium of the university. The teacher shook her head with a smile. The woman buried herself in the letter again. Probably she could not quite believe that the boy had really made it. And that he remembered her . . . She asked how many stops were left before the university. Ten minutes yet, said the teacher. Or was she a pharmacist perhaps? At any rate, I knew that she had graduated in something. The woman finally folded the letter and tucked it back into her purse. She smiled at me. I smiled back. Was I also going to the graduation ceremony? Yes, I said and blushed. Because I felt that the pharmacist was looking at me. Your brother? No, I said, my fiancé. Congratulations, the woman said and extended her bony, speckled hand. I took it. I asked if her son . . . No, my godchild! Congratulations, I said, and the pharmacist looked out the window with a superior air.

8

What did you study? the woman asked. I? Nothing. That's better anyway, she said, for a woman it's better. What do you do? Secretary, I said quickly, because it occurred to me that at least I could have learned to type. That's a good occupation for a woman, the godmother said. I am a secretary too, the pharmacist said, I'm going to see my sister receive her doctorate.

And there in the auditorium it smelled of too many people, and they spoke Latin, some men had disguised themselves and wore strange head coverings, and behind me someone said that the advanced degree in engineering is just as good as the doctorate, both are equivalent academic degrees, and I thought that Rolf not only had an advanced engineering degree but was also a Doctor of Technology. That made me feel cold, and on the evening of that Tuesday I could not make love with him anymore. His underpants were disconcerting. I had to turn away. Good night, magic. Where does love go when it goes? Into the ass? Don't be so vulgar. He was so strong, I so weak, everything so beautiful, and now I can't anymore. Don't be a child, said Rolf. How his lean body pushed itself against me that night. Go to a blind person and say: Don't be blind! All right then, the Doctor of Engineering said, and turned off the light.

Father says, Rolf is a decent and capable guy, Mother says, I can be proud of Rolf, Grandmother says, the most important thing is a respectable connection. Karl thought differently, and said nothing. But Karl hasn't really counted ever since he told a true story as a concrete example of inhumane treatment, when he was teaching the children in his school about human rights. A farmhand was hospitalized in our district, where aside from a broken leg the diagnosis was also neglect and chronic malnutrition. The farmhand was not able to form coherent sentences, he had slept in the larder, where the farmers keep their smoked meat, his food consisted of waste that he was served in the yard during the summer and in the barn during the winter, and the farmhand had never seen money, although he was a recipient of welfare, but the farmer had embezzled it, so Karl told his children at school the story about the farmhand, and I told Father, Father was just eating smoked meat, and because the farmer is a loyal patient of ours, as Mother calls it, and because we are proud of the loyalty of our customers, and perhaps the smoked meat was from the farmer, in any case Karl since then has been a psychopath and thus does not count. It is really too late to back out now. Rolf's mother and my parents are already on family terms. Grandmother got out her Bohemian crystal glasses and the lace tablecloth that afternoon when we set the date for everything, and the box with the brownish photographs, then Rolf said that I resemble my mother, and Grandmother said that my heart-shaped mouth is hers, however, she showed her teeth, all of them original, she said, that was a faux pas, because Rolf's mother has dentures, and Grandmother didn't notice that she got into more hot water when she explained where the strong teeth in our family come from, namely from her side of the family which has been healthy for generations, and I am supposed to show my teeth, and that afternoon Father gave Rolf his second pair of hip boots. Now he will have a fishing companion and a fellow hunter. There is no backing out anymore.

Who goes in first? They push me: you! With whom? With Father, of course. The organ is playing. Organists wear woolen warm-ups on their fingers, I saw that once in the movies, they are always poor and cold because they are artists. Karl isn't cold, but he drinks. People laugh at organists who compose music. Anton Bruckner[2] lived in the village where the thing with the farmhand occurred. During the nights he used up a lot of light, oil, or electricity, anyway the landlord was angry, and everybody said that Teacher Bruckner was nuts. Was he married? Give me one more kiss, says Mother. Me too, says Father. I want one more kiss too, says Grandmother, look, there is your future mother-in-law! Grandmother points her finger, Father retrieves her hand. Don't talk so much! After all, I should be allowed to talk, says Grandmother, I am the Mother, and if it were not for me none of you would be here. A photographer gets in our way. Come on, says Father. Walk straight. Don't stumble over your dress.

This is your wedding, you are the bride, what you are wearing is not a long white nightgown, it is a bridal gown. And the man who is sitting next to you so pale, that is still Rolf, your husband from now on, not as far

2. A nineteenth-century Austrian romantic composer of mostly religious works.

as you are concerned but for the others. You said Yes in front of the priest and thought No. So you lied. Now you have to lie in the bed you have made for yourself, the beautiful brass bed. Waiters are strutting around. I never could stand waiters. There is something slippery about them. They serve me first, although I sit the farthest away from the door, it's a long way, left . . . two . . . three, if you please, then it is Rolf's turn, if you please, then my mother, she isn't losing a daughter, she is gaining a son, then Rolf's mother. She has one long hair on her upper lip. When she laughs you can see her diseased gums, where she has the gold hooks. Ever since Rolf's father died of a stroke, she has laughed and talked a lot. Without interruption, really. Of course, we will not live with her. Rolf moves with the times. Left . . . two . . . three, there is another waiter. I get a slice of pineapple with a red cherry in the middle. Only I? No, I first. The order is important. How can anyone waste a thought on things like that? How can one wait table at such a wedding? Besides, it is cold. But no one admits it. This restaurant used to be the dining hall of a castle. On the walls there are still paintings that look like dirty stains. Because I am nearsighted. A bride with glasses, that won't do. It is expensive here, and Father paid for everything. How can you admit, then, that the heater doesn't work properly? Rolf doesn't notice me at all. It is his day. He just doesn't know which one. Everything went according to plan. Bought a condominium with a down payment from Mother-in-law and Father. The thing was a good buy. Capital investment. A beautiful apartment is a high-se-

curity prison. Albert and Hilde are sitting between Uncle Mandi and Aunt Grete. Hilde wanted to be a TV an-
nouncer, her parents did not allow it. So she bought
Albert with an apartment. Albert would not be able to
afford this standard of living without Hilde. So they are
even.

I like Albert better than Rolf. I have always liked him.
That will occupy my mind in the future. The meat was
excellent, someone says. Please, Waiter, don't forget the
cigars! The bride is supposed to smile. Why? Your picture is being taken, says Mother. The bride is supposed
to look this way, incline her head a little, thank you! In
England they say "Cheese!" when taking pictures,
someone says, don't you think they make too much fuss
about French cheese? When you remember that in Austria . . . at least twenty-three kinds of cheese . . . But in-
comparable! If you never were in France . . . France used
to be great, maybe! Last summer I was there, someone
says, hopeless, hope-less, I tell you. I would say, someone says, that since Pompidou no French president . . .
But I would think that under De Gaulle . . . No! De
Gaulle was never interested in . . . If you go back in history . . . Long live the bride. How young she looks, and
everything ahead of her! Not everything, ha ha. The
bride is supposed to smile once more. *When you're smiling, when you're smiling, the whole world smiles with
you.* Long live Bob Hope! The bride is tipsy. Bob who? Bob
Hope, the American film star! Wrong, Bob Hope was
English, someone says. Why "was"? The bride is tipsy.

Now I really must see what Uncle Mandi's wedding

present is. He slipped the envelope into my hand in the vestry. Probably Aunt Grete isn't supposed to know that he is giving me money. Uncle Mandi made a special trip from Lunz am See and has . . . please put that away . . . and he has given me . . . put that envelope away immediately . . . Uncle Mandi did not mind the long way from Lunz am See in order to . . . if you don't put away that envelope this moment I'll slap you later, says Rolf. Three thousand shillings. Aunt Grete is wearing a hat with a brim. That would have been a good idea. Why didn't I get married with a hat on? I have a face made for a hat. Anyway, you are not allowed to slap me, Rolf, because I am the bride, and after all Karl has already slapped me, as you know very well. Thank you, Karl, that you thought of me the day before the wedding, you didn't forget me. You know, Rolf, when you fought about me with Karl in front of the school, Karl was right, I had lied to you. Why aren't you interested in that, you should be interested in what kind of person you married. No, says Rolf, I'm not interested. Everybody is eating. Everybody is having coffee. I will take a picture of the photographer. But Rolf is against it. The waiter has brought the cigars. There is a paper bow on every cigar showing Grossglockner Peak. Is it the custom at Austrian weddings that the highest mountain must be one of the party? Everybody pretends that they are used to drinking wine at weddings. Today's guests are the same that ate with us at Grandfather's funeral. So we meet again. The photographer is still taking pictures. With every flash Father gets stomach cramps. He is the one who gets the bill. Even the photographer got his meal as if he were part of the family. Probably so that he wouldn't take pictures without interruption. Father is shrewd. You are drunk, says Rolf, aren't you ashamed of yourself? Albert has a birthmark on his chin. I am not drunk enough not to see that. Karl once said that among all the other students Albert was the only one you were not ashamed to sit in the same classroom with. What did Karl mean by that?

All congratulatory telegrams say the same thing. So many people who don't like us wish us happiness. No one came up with something special, not even those who like us. Rolf read every telegram out loud. Now we must be happy, how could we not be. The room is on the fourth floor. You can't hear yourself walking on these carpets. A man comes towards us. He kisses my hand. Actually I have to go to the bathroom very urgently. He says that his wife is happy for us. How does he know that? The man appreciates Rolf, and so he pulls my hand towards his mouth again. Finally alone. Rolf lets me go ahead into the room. It smells new. Was the hotel built for us? Why do we have to go to a hotel anyway? Rolf disappears into the bathroom. He closes the door behind him. The hotel rooms I am familiar with don't have baths, just tiny sinks, shabby armchairs, view of dark backyards, moaning of emigrants, I have read too many novels, anyway, I am hungry. I don't like it here. I want to go down and eat something. We just got married, however, so I cannot go down alone.

In the dining room Rolf caresses my hand. I caress the

napkin. He takes the lighter from my hand because he has to light my cigarette. You're smoking before dinner? I put out the cigarette. Why do I smoke before dinner? Rolf is right. Go ahead and smoke, he says, you are free. Of course, I am free. I take the lighter and a cigarette. Rolf again takes the lighter from my hand. Delay of six seconds. Why doesn't he reach for the lighter before I have it in my hands? Actually, I wanted to marry Laurence Olivier. You're not eating again! At an adjoining table food is sent back. The waiter carries the tray past us. Rolf nods somehow in solidarity. But to whom is he loyal?

You were not so hungry after all, he says, when we take the elevator upstairs. Then we look for our room. Does he still remember which number it is? If we don't find the room he will file a missing room report. But Rolf finds the number very easily, pushes me through the door, locks up behind me, stands next to me, no, he isn't leaving, he is getting undressed. Behind the drapes there is probably a window. I saw blackbirds when we got out of the car. Are they cold in the snow? Why did we actually have to get married in the winter? It is so cold that I have to take a bath. Rolf says that taking a bath on a full stomach is not good for you. But I ate so little. Who died of a nosebleed on his wedding night? King Attila! I remember that from my history class because the most smart-alecky fellow in the class said to the teacher: Of course, he had to stick his nose into everything! He was later expelled because he spoke too often without being called on. Maybe Rolf will have a heart attack while I take a bath. I get undressed slowly. A bomb could go off in the hotel. Nowadays there are bombs everywhere. Nice thought that someone before me used these towels. And many people after me will use them. If you let yourself glide into the bath water very slowly it tickles nicely on your dry skin. I stay until the water gets cold. I rub myself with the towels until my skin is red all over. What can I do now to make him fall asleep? The bathrobe that my mother-in-law had ordered for me has long ties. You can tie them in the front or in the back. Whichever way you want. There you are finally, he says, and quickly reaches for the gift with a bow. He lets his hand grope, unwraps, asks if he may turn on the light, deposits pointed kisses on my skin that cannot defend itself, for when a woman does not want to be kissed she has to give extensive reasons, and when she has finished with that she gets a kiss for it because it is so touching when women try hard to explain something because a woman is a woman. Men simply say no, and when they don't want to they are also not able to. I say: No. The game begins. Why not? Because I am unhappy, Rolf. He turns on the light, looks at me and contends that unhappy people look different. I turn off the light. He turns it on. Kisses me on my nose because it is turned up, and snub-noses cry outright to be snubbed and kissed. And all the things I say this night, don't touch me, let me sleep, I don't want to, I would rather go for a walk alone right now, without you, all that doesn't count because Rolf turns on the light again and again and looks at me, and snub-noses can say whatever they want, they look as they look, before and afterwards, and his hand goes on groping, I shoo it away, he says, he has imagined this differently, the bed creaks, now I cannot say no any longer, after all he is a man of flesh and blood, and I shout: No! He is lying next to me again, his heart is thumping, I can hear it, I am afraid that he will cry, then I will be wet with his tears. I know, I have burdened myself with a serious guilt, and maybe starting tomorrow he will help me divide this guilt between us and gradually I will become freer so that we can breathe again, together.

The room is still there when I open my eyes, the weight on my chest, this dry air. I sneak to the curtain, there really is a window, and there is fresh snow outside, it must have snowed. Amazing that this day has simply come. That the sky is still there. Something in the room is moving now. It is Rolf. His eyes are moist with yawning. He lifts himself on his elbows. Good morning! Good morning! He extends his arm towards me, and his pajamas are blue, with dark blue stripes, and a little pocket on the upper left side. Why do pajamas have these little pockets? He smiles. Come! He continues extending his arm, imploring, friendly, drowsy, devoted, and I put my hand into his warm, dry hand. He pulls me down to him, I let myself be pulled. He lifts me into bed. I let myself be lifted. He pushes my nightgown up. I let him strip me completely. Because I am outside in the snow, with the blackbirds, because I will not be here when you touch me.

Birds of death and moonfish breasts. I knew that he meant crows and ravens. But what did the moonfish breasts in Karl's poems mean? Why did he sit there and read me poems that he had written, although I did not understand a word?

Believe me, life can be beautiful, said Karl, and read and read. He was six years older than I was, like Rolf, and I wanted to believe everything that older people told me. For at eighteen I had started feeling sadness and I did not know where it came from, and I went to see Karl to tell him about it. He put on a serious face, ignored the hot chestnuts that I had brought, got some typed manuscripts from his drawers, and then he read those poems to me. There were a lot of foreign words in them, too, which I didn't understand, but I didn't dare to ask because Karl took me seriously, and we sat next to each other for a whole afternoon. I began feeling ashamed of myself because of the urge I had immediately felt when I came in: to touch Karl's neck, to make something happen between him and me, and the longer he read the less comfortable it was to sit there with our bodies close together. Maybe I was too young for his taste. As a lady I could not just kiss him. I told Rolf about that later, and Rolf touched my neck instead of answering my questions about Karl, and then it happened with Rolf, and I had good reason to feel contempt for Karl with his moonfish breasts. And this is probably the way it began. Rolf laughed with me when I started laughing at Karl. That bound us together.

Everything was simpler with Rolf. The women conductors in the street cars were friendlier when I got on with Rolf. When I went to the theater with Rolf the ticket sellers smiled. When the sadness returned Rolf said that it had to do with my insecurity. On those afternoons I spent crying on the couch while he was making drawings of his screws, that sight of personified usefulness consoled me. When he had finished his drawing he sat down with me and was my mother. He spoke of the pleasant aspects of the century in which we live, turned on the radio until we had the right music, was happy when I swallowed my last tears, and said that life had me in its grip again, and I didn't tell him that the music had accomplished that, not he. Because he was happy when I was happy, and when I read to him from my diary that my skin hurt all over with yearning for his skin, then he said that he wanted children with me and with no other woman. Everything was all right with Rolf. And when the sadness returned, he said, maybe you inherited an inclination to depression, and now you simply have to live with it.

Honeymoon as planned. A trip to the South. It would have been impossible to call off the wedding since, after all, the invitations had been printed. Such beautiful ones, too. Double cards, you can open and close them. To call off the wedding, that would be like calling off a funeral because the dead person suddenly is not dead at all. After having begun to mourn, now you are supposed to be happy again? Of course, we'll go to Italy. Lago di Garda. It was long ago when I filled crackling little bags with pebbles, those days with Father and Mother, when we stayed the night in Riva, in the evening people drove their sheep through town, we used the little sugar bags from the coffeehouse, now I remember, and Mother had brownish red hair, she stooped down, leave those pebbles alone, said Father, do let the child play, said Mother. Maybe Mother spoiled me too much? And the story of the ring buoy. I absolutely had to have one. Father didn't talk either to Mother or to me any more. But I got it. Then I didn't want it anymore and threw it away. But Rolf is not a buoy. His stomach nerves are delicate and he throws up after breakfast. Maybe it's because he sticks his toothbrush too far down in his mouth. No, if you want to know: I've been feeling sick the whole night. Are you sick? I didn't sleep all night! Are we going home? You would like that, wouldn't you, he said. One does not cut a honeymoon short.

While Rolf couldn't sleep, I dreamed that the justice of the peace said to me: You cannot get married, wait a minute! He came and wanted to remove a thorn from my arm. It was a long black stalk that sprayed out water when he snapped it. We must pull it out, he said to Rolf, but Rolf was in a hurry and didn't want to wait. I tore at the thorn, suddenly there was a hole in my arm. It's not over yet! the man shouted, and now it was no longer the justice of the peace, but the pastor. Pull hard! he shouted, and I pulled and pulled and pulled, and then there was a plant in my arm, with blossoms, stamens, and I pulled and pulled and pulled, and there were new blossoms, they looked like fruity thistles, and it didn't stop, and I had to pull again and again, and I woke up exhausted, and Rolf was lying awake next to me. Then the justice of the peace raised his book, made a speech of which he was very proud, and he showed us that he had written it with a fountain pen, it was a clear handwriting as if engraved, and Grandmother was standing behind me, and she said, this is a likable, decent handwriting. And Rolf had not gotten any sleep!

Red, yellow, ochre houses, mountains with snow and blue sky, Brescia, Milano, how nice that sounds: Milano. As a child I used to sing it to myself, Milano, I want to be a child again. Rolf knows his way around here. He was in Milan several times. And we arrive in Genoa. Rolf explains everything worth knowing about the harbor and its economic significance. Finally Florence. Florence sounds better than Firenze. Rolf thinks so too. I am happy about that. One should have lived here five hundred years ago. That would have been a good life. Rolf doesn't think so. He is listening to the history of the Pontevecchio from a machine that you activate with one hundred lire. He is hurt that I don't want to listen to that story. Then it starts raining. That upsets him even more. Although the rain makes the Arno quite yellow and the sky so low, everything dipped in color. Michelangelo used to walk over these cobblestones, barefoot. Did you think they didn't have shoes in those days? asks Rolf. Perhaps Michelangelo once put his hand on this door latch. A small, secret happiness. I sneak fragments of pleasure out of Rolf's day. In the hotel there is a TV set, Cary Grant and Grace Kelly are swimming in it. Millions are at stake. Rolf wants to see the story. He scrubs my back in the bathtub, and it occurs to him that my toes are too big for my small feet. I say, those toes are good for walking. And good night! No, he says, I didn't mean anything.

Italy is a boot. We are driving down the zipper. You can see the Appenines over there. Dear. What is it like actually in the Appenine Mountains? Not interesting. Why? Otherwise we would hear about it, if there was anything interesting there. That's true. In geography class we merely learned: Appenine. And that was it. Are the Italians true descendants of the Romans? Sure, Rolf says. He knows. And also knows how to read road maps, how you handle gasoline stamps, that the Italians are crooks. La strada. Le strade. You want to learn Italian? Why not, una birra, due birre. Oh, stop it, that's not a language. Uomo avvisato, mezzo salvato! Quando nacqui, mi disse una voce: tu sei nato a portare la tua croce.[3] Are you trying to annoy me? Where did you get this book? You better learn Spanish, there is a future in that!

But Rome, Rome, finally to Rome! Grandmother told stories about the catacombs and about the porter who knows her personally to this day. Every year she writes a postcard before she goes to Sicily, then the porter picks her up at her train compartment in Rome. Every year she takes a carton of cigarettes for him. And Grandmother saw all three popes, and she received a blessing from all of them. She liked Pope Pius the best. In Rome every-

3. Translation of the Italian phrases: The street. The streets. . . . One beer, two beers. . . . Forewarned is forearmed! When I was born a voice said to me: you are born to bear your cross.

thing is different, Grandmother said, because it is the Eternal City. But Rolf has a little booklet that says where you have to go in Rome. We imagined St. Peter's Cathedral was bigger. Now we are getting along fine again. Rolf, do you think that the pope has a girl friend? Possibly. Does he have one or doesn't he? Probably, Rolf says. That's not all I've heard about the pope, but I can see that Rolf is not interested in such things because it was in a French sex magazine. And the cardinals? All atheists, Rolf says, the Church is politics like everything else! Why don't we leave the Church then? Rolf says, because there are no advantages to that. Why actually did we get married in church? Rolf says, as an Austrian you are Catholic, and you wear that like a national costume. And that's it now, we have to go to the Spanish Steps. Well, I don't have to. May I ask why not? No, I want to ask why you always talk like those stupid grade school teachers. Karl says that even the twenty-year-olds say: Those young people nowadays! Karl once heard the beginning of a conversation among young colleagues, and he thought they were parodying the grade school principal, who always wears a national costume too, and then he noticed that they were saying exactly what they thought. He was confused by that. Will you come to the Spanish Steps, please? He doesn't get an answer and crosses the street with quick, annoyed footsteps. The camera with which he dispatched the Colosseum is dangling from his shoulder. If it were summer he would wear a little cap and shorts. Then you would be able to see his thin legs. He got diarrhea from eating risotto. He is angry at Italy. But I want to stay in the Colosseum and not run away from the horror, I want to understand what was allowed to happen here, after all it says that nothing happens without God wanting it, and where were omnipotence and mercy when those gladiators attacked each other? What did the men and women who were looking on think? What did they feel? What has changed since then? Nothing at all has changed. The history and geography teacher's mouth always watered when he said: Brazil, coffee, Colombia, bananas, and the battle at, and the execution of, and he always dwelled leisurely on Napoleon and Bismarck because otherwise he would have had to discuss Austria under the German regime, and there he never knew what to say, as a teacher on the one hand, as a member of the party on the other hand. Nothing has changed, only customs change, and the air I breathe also passed through the lungs of the gladiators, I am sitting on blood and in blood, and blood runs through the body of the postcard vendor. Why isn't this a temple? Here is where I would be able to pray. Not over there under the dome. This is where there is truth, not in those frescoes.

If the Italians hadn't changed their colors, Rolf says, we wouldn't have lost the war. The German soldiers were the bravest, and unfortunately Adolf Hitler didn't listen to his generals, and you don't have to be a Nazi or a Fascist to see things differently from what we are forced to believe nowadays. After all, who hanged the Russian and the English and the French war criminals? No, no, he says, you have to become more mature if I am to talk

25

politics with you. And he doesn't want spaghetti, neither Milanese nor Bolognese style, and Italian women all have legs that are too short and hips that are too broad, and they don't even know German, and on the beach the wind is blowing, everything bleak all around, the sky is like a sailcloth above water of steel. Whoever sees the sea first gets an ice cream cone, Father says. Me, I see the sea! Why is there salt in the sea? Mother laughs. The fishermen take their boats out, Father says, and they have these packages, and they scatter the salt carefully in the waves. Mother laughs and caresses me. Mother and Father are happy, I believe. You are frigid, says Rolf, I don't know, I say, because one quickly gets used to saying: I don't know. But he wants to know why I find everything beautiful that he finds ugly, and vice versa, and why I don't let him take my picture, why I am stubborn and contrary. I can't say anything because he squeezes flat whatever I confide to him. He gives me back only the peel: see, this is how empty your contention was. Say something else, I will examine it. See, again it's nothing. There you can have it back. And don't always think of your stupid childhood, deal with the present, grow up at last. How does one grow up? Don't worry, I'll teach you. Rolf, when I was a child I was looking forward to being an adult. I was full of expectation and impatience. Every birthday was a victory! And now I want to go back, I want to return to my mother's womb, when I look at us. What is the matter with us, Rolf asks, why do you draw me into your moods? I am enjoying this trip!

You'll be able to see that in the photographs, later, when we go through the album and show it, then we'll understand that we had a beautiful honeymoon like every sensible couple. We do look quite normal on the outside. The sun and the sea, how it all sparkles, the white hotels, the transparent stones, the red trash baskets. Rolf stops the car in order to empty the ashtray into such a trash basket. I want to be able to talk to someone without being set straight. To the trash basket! Lie down in the street and talk to the street. Do stop crying! It feels good, Rolf. Then cry, if it feels good. But don't cry endlessly, he says, you are already all puffed up! I think of how the human body consists to a great extent of water and that perhaps you can cry yourself away, and clothes, shoes, purse, and everything that must be considered valuable items stay behind on the car seat, and Rolf can gather them up, and that's the end of misunderstandings for him.

Maybe you always thought of yourself as something special, he says, after all you were spoiled by your parents, your childhood was happy, so life isn't what you imagined it to be, and so now you have difficulties.

I was a special child. I wore a green coat with round buttons, we were walking along a green path, Mother and I, to a house with smaller windows, with people who were unlike us, they were poorer people who recognized immediately that it was an honor to be allowed to receive my mother and me because we were affiliated with Father, and Father was the most important man in town, he cured everybody, he saved many people's lives. People were divided into two groups: our patients, the good people, and not our patients, the bad ones. I knew that besides the people there was something else, the doctors, and my friends were doctors' children, we went to medical conventions in Italy, and it was something special to have an earache because then Father came upstairs from his office in his white coat and occupied himself with me, even though it hurt when he pressed the cotton balls into my ears, but they were Father's hands, and when Father caused me pain it was right, and I was proud that he noticed me whenever I had an earache. And when I registered at the university in Vienna no one knew my father, which astonished me very much, I was no longer myself, just anybody, I was one among so many, that hurt, and then Rolf came, who recognized me, he knew who I was, and I had to sleep with him because it was all so right. Do you think that's it, Rolf? Yes, he said, and you know how much esteem I have for your father. Your parents love you, and me too, so we can't disappoint them. They expected you to finish a major, to do something, to set goals for yourself, and you offended them. Your marriage was your parents' last hope. Don't you think, Rolf, that I'm somehow perverse? You are just immature! How does one become mature? You mature gradually, he says, and then he takes my picture with and without scarf, then both of us with the self-timer, and he says that he can go far in his job. How far? For example, I can become president of VOEST!⁴ Really? With

4. VOEST is a major Austrian company engaged in metallurgy, engineering, and contracting.

your support I will reach any goal, no matter how high.

A woman needs a man, and we are doing fine. He will climb the ladder higher and higher, I will hold the ladder so that it won't tip over. We will have children, but only our own since with adoption, he says, you never know what kind of hereditary material gets into the family. A woman without a man, what kind of thing is that? He is stronger. But then she can bear children. And whether blood circulation, liver, and kidneys enable us to live a meaningful life, or whether we have to live according to the dictates of blood circulation, liver, and kidneys, those are questions which we shouldn't ask ourselves. Where would we be if we turned everything around? Brooding doesn't do any good. You should be happy to be alive. Other children would be happy, if they. . . .

Since I've never been in a casino, Rolf indulges me, and he exchanges five hundred shillings. When those five hundred are used up we quit, agreed? Agreed. Although. But Rolf knows the story of my other grandfather whom we don't speak about because he gambled away several houses. We go gambling. For the first time, since the wedding, we. Our passports are examined, nobody notices that we are here only for fun, we must sign a statement that we are not employed by the casino and that we renounce forever the right to work in this casino. The croupiers have beautiful faces. Maybe every face is beautiful when it is serious?

Rolf guides me from table to table. After all, dogs in the park have to be kept on a leash, too. Rolf explains Red and Black, Even and Odd, that's child's play, he explains the special thing about the Zero, so I want to bet on Zero, but Rolf says, Zero doesn't make sense, you don't bet on numbers at all if you have as little money as we do, then Zero comes up, I knew it, I am not at all surprised, and now of course Seventeen, I know that Seventeen will come, Seventeen stands out among all the numbers, I know that now Seventeen will come! Rolf doesn't want to get into a fight again, nor me either, so I don't bet. The Seventeen comes up. Hats off to the gambler! What is someone like Rolf doing here? He goes from one table to the next, always playing it safe. Whatever he bets here he gets back there. I hate him. He finds me ungrateful, and we sneak out, after all you have to be ashamed of yourself with someone like Rolf among real gamblers.

Back via Genoa, Milan. There is no Milano. In Florence I should have hidden, if I had only thought of it in time. Michelangelo lived on bread, wine, and cheese. That was before the invention of vitamins. In the mountains sheep are grazing, lizards are flitting across rocks, you see their shimmering green.

Occupation: housewife, it says in my new passport. They should have written snail. Snail. Hair: dyed. Eyes: brown. Distinguishing marks: none, it says in the passport. What a mistake. You just can't see them at first sight. Distinguishing marks: sloppy, unfair, ungrateful, unable, unrealistic, unhappy, unsatisfied, lazy, insolent. Setting the table, clearing the table, washing the dishes, shopping, cooking, setting the table, clearing the table. Washing the dishes. What shall I cook for dinner, three hundred and sixty-five times a year the question: What shall I cook for dinner? To be or not to be, whether 'tis nobler, how much are the tomatoes today? But you're supposed to know that, whether tomatoes are in season or not. Of course, we have money, but it's particularly important for those who have money to learn to manage well, it's not beneath you to show some interest in that, go to the marketplace, compare the prices and the sales, you yourself admit that you are bored, call Hilde, she can advise you, Hilde would be a good friend for you, make friends with my friends' wives! He is right, he brings home the money, knows what the Israelis are doing wrong with the Arabs, knows why the strikes in England are still going on, knows what he has to do and therefore what I have to do, but in return I am frigid, justice must be upheld.

The greengrocer bows. Madame Diplomingenieur, please, thank you, Frau Doktor, I kiss your hand, Auf Wiedersehen! May I hold the door for Madame? I am not me. I am Rolf's wife. Nobody used to hold doors for me. I never used to buy vegetables either. They hold the doors for my mother everywhere too. Grandmother says, that's the way it is when you are the wife of a VIP. The delicatessen owner and his wife always receive my mother with special kindness. She is so absentminded. Wants to buy milk, and the delicatessen owner stands at the cash register, where he miscalculates so often, gulps when he talks about all those things that have come in fresh again for Herr Doktor, capers, very big, Spanish shells in a very delicate sauce, and my mother takes everything because the owner's wife has already started filling the basket, anything for the Herr Doktor, who has such gourmet taste, and Mother takes home the fresh bananas and the special meat and everything that has just come in fresh, and the merchant runs up the bill voluptuously, and most of the time Mother has to send the charwoman later because she forgot to get what she had set out to buy, and she can't stand up to the delicatessen owner, after all he is a private patient, and she even has to buy venison there sometimes, although Father shoots his own deer and sometimes even gets it for free from the game store, because the delicatessen owner's wife's cousin had a falling out with the delicatessen owner, and she gives us game meat on purpose so that he can't sell his. We should play the families off against each other much more, Rolf's mother said, but my mother doesn't even realize that anything is being played. She is just amazed that she always comes home so loaded down when all she did was run out of milk.

And which laundry detergent? Do I have to buy Maresi today because it is written with chalk on the blackboard under "Announcements"? Today Maresi is cheaper, only until tomorrow. I understand now the meaning of advertising. There are so many sales, and you have to be able to decide freely. That is a science. Lettuce isn't always the same price either, and there is a season for peppers and seasons in which you don't buy peppers. I knew so little. For example I didn't know that you rinse off the cutting board with water before you cut onions. Grandmother told me: so that no odor remains in the wood. Always only a pinch of thyme, rosemary, cinnamon, marjoram, cloves, one should not taste them clearly, crush garlic with the back of a knife, always with salt, and peel it first, of course, and use a broad knife for the garlic, and don't throw lemons away after squeezing them, always keep lemons in reach for dirty hands. The housewife's hand shouldn't show that it has been working. Put parsley in a glass of water, learn to economize, and no canned goods, says Grandmother, all that is poison, use only natural things, soft soap is the best soap, keep old bread for crumbs, put everything in little bags, with clear labels on them. At night I go to sleep with the cookbook that she gave me. It is a respectable collection of recipes from the national institute for teachers of home economics and from the cooking school for innkeepers in Vienna. An indispensable help and reference work for the managers and employees of domestic or wholesale small or big kitchens, that's what it says on the yellowed jacket.

At the lunch table, always the big meal of the day, there was always a certain nervousness noticeable in my mother's voice and gestures after my father had sat down at the table. Mother took the pieces of meat from the pan. I handed her Father's plate. Muttering. Small irritation. Doubts, hesitancy. This piece for Father? No, the lean one for Father. He doesn't like fat. Who says I don't like fat? Why isn't there any soup? Well, says Mother, if I make soup along with meat like this you ask why I made soup. And when I don't then you ask why I didn't make any! A spoonful of soup wouldn't be bad, Father then said diffidently, and Mother would feel guilty. The sword of Damocles was always hovering over her, and that is how it always was at lunchtime, and resignation when Father didn't finish, helplessness and despair when he pushed back his plate without a word and then declared that he wasn't hungry. However, at meals when Father was in a good mood we got the same thing laced with witty remarks. The glider! First Mother defended herself. It wasn't her fault that the goose was too thin. And too old. You just left it in the oven too long and didn't baste it enough. All right then, let's eat. Mother cut up the dry pieces, the word glider came up again and again, and when Mother realized that Father had forgiven her long ago she joined the laughter and we had wine, and there were other jokes: Is this a duck? No, a goose. A glider? When Father felt like it he was magically able to produce a lot of happiness in Mother's face.

Do put that book down, Rolf says, you don't learn cooking from books, you learn it from experience. Flaky puff pastry is his favorite dish. Onion soup is the only soup I can actually cook. He doesn't like onion soup. And nothing has happened yet today. I've just been waiting. After supper the day was really over. I took the dishes to the kitchen, rolled up the tablecloth and shook it out over the railing of the kitchen balcony. I have it good. Other women don't have a kitchen balcony. Rolf puts his arm under my neck, he comes closer, it is so quiet, everything so black and quiet, he comes without a face, but I know that it is he, I can't, yet he can. If nature had made men as hypersensitive as women then the human race would have died out long ago. Now he is sleeping well, even if I wasn't lobster for him, just hamburger.

How he drops the sugar into his cup, stirs, puts the spoon on the plate, raises the cup, drinks, how he polishes his glasses and puts them on, carries the cup to the kitchen, lets the water run, rinses out the cup, how he takes his coat and his briefcase, unlocks the door and closes it behind him, and how much time I have now to watch that, every morning.

Once, yes, I wanted something, wanted to do something, I was from a good home, I would always have a good home and be good, everything was all right, how we lived, what Father and Mother did, they each did their duty, and I learned to read and write, in preschool it had been so boring, but grade school was highly interesting, and then high school graduation. Everything was laid out and well planned. After you graduate life begins. But what do you do with so much freedom? One semester you get for free, said Father, loaf around, look around in Vienna, and then decide. But let me tell you one thing right now, said Father, the only really satisfying field is medicine. So it's Medicine then. And not actress or saleswoman or journalist. Medicine is the way, and here I lose it because it's impossible for me to use the corpses in the dissecting room as objects of learning. I can't do it, digging out the right intestine among all the intestines in the belly, I can't skin the skull of the old woman that is lying on the table, I see only yellow feet and shrouds, I don't like the students' jokes, the students don't like me either, they call me the virgin from the provinces, so now what do you want to do, said Father, I'm waiting for your decision. Maybe translator. Father is disappointed. After all, we already practiced the signature, my first name and the last name that I got from my father together with the doctor's title, we practiced that one whole evening, how you best combine my future title with my first name in one elegant line. My first name has an awkward initial, it took us a long time before we could agree, and Father said I should combine the doctor's title directly with my last name, and then add my first initial at the end.

As a translator you don't get a doctorate, only a diploma. Are you satisfied with that? Suddenly I had slipped into the lower classes. When I would sit with my colleagues they would call me a colleague. Could I be a part of them? They were all second class. They wanted to translate at conferences and just repeat what others had said. Without a doctorate. How could one want to live like that? So I registered for German. We chopped up a poem by Goethe according to metric rules. Then it occurred to me that Goethe didn't need German metrics to write his poem. What did Goethe study? So then it was law. Then Rolf comes into the picture, loves me and thinks a woman has no prospects anyway, something feminine would be best. I would like to become an actress. Acting is too uncertain. Something practical. A teacher. No, I don't want to be a teacher. Why not? I can't possibly stand in front of the children and pretend to know more than they do. I cannot possibly teach thirty children at one time. What other occupations are there in which a woman has a future without giving up being a true woman? That's so difficult. Maybe painting? Not practical. Yes, you do nice drawings, you should keep that up, but as a hobby. Keep in mind, my child: Don't ever make your hobby into your job. That really spoils it for you. Rolf always used to have so much interest in building radios and constructing ships. Then he was studying technology and he got fed up with it. So at least he wanted to get the doctorate in addition to his diploma to make the whole thing more exciting again.

I realized that I lack the little motor which everybody else had built in, I am missing something really important, which makes others so fast and hard-working. Ambition? But there was a time when I did want to do something. I was eager to learn, and at some point in high school that stopped, at some point the motor fell out, and I didn't listen any more when the Latin teacher explained something, I just wondered at the ruins he had in his mouth, and whether his wife could stand it when he kisses her, whether she isn't disgusted by so much saliva and odor, and then I was not promoted for the first time. Not outwardly. I got to graduate somehow by fraud, it couldn't have happened honestly that I suddenly wore the black robe and the black top hat like all the others, that I made the rounds of the town on the cart as one graduate among all the other graduates of that year. Deep inside I was not promoted. And Rolf took the dough and kneaded it until it was pliable. Off to the oven, bake it, and suddenly they are serious about the wedding and the business of real life.

You must study, says Gerlinde, our graduating class was not a valid year, none of us earned the graduation diploma, we must redo our assignments and the exams, but I've forgotten everything. You must learn it again, says Gerlinde, after all I gave you so many private lessons! Were you really so stupid or did you just pretend, you must get your high school diploma, what will your parents say if you come home without your diploma, but I forgot everything, yet Gerlinde is standing next to me, she is a school girl, she has everything in her notebook and also in her head. Then we are in a youth hostel, Gerlinde has to go to the doctor, she isn't feeling well, she returns and says that somebody tried to poison her food, I am under suspicion, the Latin teacher is my counsel, he listens to what I say, I say that I dislike Gerlinde although she is my best friend and helper in Latin, but I wish her dead. I say I would have been happy had she been poisoned, yet it wasn't me who put poison in her food, I swear it, and the Latin teacher remains neutral, he says the subject matter is the important thing, and I say I'm not afraid to be convicted because I'm happy that someone had the courage to poison Gerlinde. But if Gerlinde dies Rolf dies too, don't you know that, someone says, and then I wake up, and after such dreams Rolf would lie beside me, and it was lucky that he was still breathing and I could hold on to him, and Gerlinde is a student of Latin and German somewhere, soon she herself will be a teacher, my children will have it good with her, since we were always such good friends.

asdf jkl; asdf jkl; I will practice that with my little finger and my ring finger and my index finger and also my middle finger which is so awkward because it is too long, but Rolf's birthday is coming up, and then I'll surprise him with my typing skills.

I practice on Grandfather's typewriter, in Grandmother's kitchen, no one disturbs us there, here Grandfather would cut his apple with his pocket knife, black bread and an apple for his afternoon snack. Grandmother says that Grandfather was able to type blind, she checked it herself by dictating the names of the streets and covering his eyes, and in the beginning she thought that he was cheating, but then he showed her that it is as easy as playing piano, but that didn't convince her since she could never really understand how you could play piano either. He was a strange person. In the yard he had a box with a tomato plantation, and he watered it every day, not too much and not too little, and around noontime he liked sitting outside to watch it grow, and one day he found a plant bare of fruit. There were only two, says Grandmother, and after all tomatoes are for eating. Grandfather was angry because he had put something else into those love apples, you don't call them tomatoes, they are love apples, Grandfather shouted, since that was the time when people in the city started saying tomatoes for love apples, and Grandmother to this day doesn't understand why he grew the tomatoes if she wasn't allowed to eat them. There is still the coal stove, and above the dining table there is a calendar from the Society for the Prevention of Cruelty to Animals and a calendar from the sos children's village. Framed photographs of my three uncles who were killed in the war. Everything is all right here, and there must be a higher power, Grandmother says, a higher purpose and an afterlife, otherwise her sons' deaths would have no meaning. Grandmother gets up every morning at six, washes herself thoroughly, doesn't want to use the modern bathroom, she has her china washbowl and her washcloth, she confesses her sins which are always the same, that is, gluttony and sometimes meat on Fridays. The priest knows that already and he gives her absolution even when she is just beginning to tell how much she ate on Sunday although she was already full. The priest said recently that meat on Fridays is no longer a sin, but she still confesses it just to be on the safe side. Once a month she takes communion, prays for Father and Mother because they are nonbelievers, now for Rolf and me also, and then she makes lunch, then the whole house smells so good that Father is disappointed when he sits down at his own table because it was Grandmother's goulash that he smelled. And after the meal she lies down, sleeps well, isn't bothered by the noise from the street, she says you get used to that like the dog gets used to beatings, and on the white sideboard there are bowls with holy water from Lourdes, and she also saw the Mater Dolorosa once on one of her trips to her Sicilian friend Amalie, the one who always writes her letters with so many spelling errors; but a good soul. Grandmother's kitchen windows look out over the yard. The sky has a different color every day, and if you can hear the bells of St. John's Church the weather will stay bad. On the icebox there are china pears in a china basket on a doily because everything must be protected. In the evening she sits down in the wing-back armchair in our TV–living room, which Father called the gentlemen's room and later the library, but we just simply call it the TV–living room— there she rests her feet, strapped into woolen slippers, on a footstool, hears and sees terrible things from different worlds, thanks the Lord for the contented life she has, although in those days, afterwards, how do you say, yes, after the capitulation, she did have to run the Russian club in the coffeehouse. Grandfather still did have the coffeehouse in those days, didn't he? And Grandmother says, when they called me on the phone I asked them about the Russian club, if that was an honor for me or a punishment. But they didn't do anything to me. The Russian occupiers ate without napkins, and only the more intelligent ones used silverware, she says, the other Russians threw the gnawed-off bones over their shoulders onto the floor. The Yugoslav prisoner of war to this day writes a postcard to her every Christmas. He had to help with Grandfather's mineral water production because the men were all at the front. Once she visited the Yugoslav in his new hometown. His own people didn't accept him any more because he had run towards the Germans with his arms raised up. His friends were partisans, says Grandmother, so Duzan had a hard time with them. His wife was already with another guy, and she said: Kill him, that traitor. But Duzan was just a poor tailor. Grandmother always treated her personnel so well that all those who are still alive like to come and see her even now. And in the bank she has twenty thousand shillings, nobody knows that. She has saved them. Later I will get them minus funeral expenses, and also the ring that Grandfather bought for her. When the time comes, she says, and don't say anything because Aunt Grete is waiting for the ring. As I said, my life has been like a novel, says Grandmother, and Father also says that his life was a novel, and Mother also says: My life was a novel. I want to know from Grandmother whether Grandfather didn't sometimes get on her nerves. He always sharpened his pencils really well, she says, and put one next to the other, saved every eraser, and everything had permanent value for him, there was no waste, Grandfather was a character. But hot-tempered. Once she locked the bedroom door from the inside by mistake and didn't find the key right away, so he immediately kicked in the door with his boot.

Grandmother has a little casket in which there is a note on top. All my special letters: To be read with devotion, only then can you burn them. All I found were some pads for adding up checks from her coffeehouse days, underneath those was Grandfather's handwriting, barely legible now, he used a hard violet pencil. He writes that he wants to apologize for something because he still needs Grandmother. A letter which I wrote to Santa Claus and in which I pretend to want a picture of a guardian angel. I wrote that only to make a good impression on Grandmother since I often heard her try to persuade my parents to put me in a convent boarding school. Dear Santa, I wrote, please when you come to Linz some time, take my big doll to the doll doctor. I would be happy to have a picture of a guardian angel to hang above my bed. Silent night, holy night, I added and pasted a pastel-colored picture of the Holy Family on their flight from Herod on the envelope. I didn't like playing with dolls, somehow they all broke. One of those times when I was taking apart a doll Grandmother said: She is not a girl. So I wrote about the doll doctor, and I had already seen Santa through the keyhole, also the real stork in the forbidden books from the doctor's office, but Grandmother was greatly impressed by my letter, and so was I. I would much rather have wished short hair for myself, but I had to have braids because my mother wanted long hair when she was a child but her mother felt it was necessary to cut off everything that had grown every month.

Other letters are from Sicily. From Amalie, Grandmother's friend from grade school days. Amalie was the child of a woman from the Steiermark and an Italian laborer. She was sent to Sicily to manage the household of a landowner. The landowner and his wife were unable to have children, so he had three children by the house-keeper. When the wife died he married the housekeeper so that he would be able to make his children his heirs. And then died on the spot. The children were his heirs and kept the mother as a housekeeper. Grandmother thinks that's a scandal. She goes to Sicily every year to prevent Mali from signing those declarations that they put in front of her while they hide her glasses.

Did you sign anything again? Grandmother asks as soon as she arrives, and Amalie first denies it, then she confesses. Grandmother looks everywhere to find the evidence. But the landowner's sons are attorneys, and you can never prove anything against them. Grand-mother also brings the right medication for her friend, for diabetes, water in her feet, arthritis; and vitamin pills for all the poor skinny dogs that roam around the house. Father has a new pharmaceutical product for arterio-sclerosis, he wanted to try it, and he sent it along with Grandmother when she went to Sicily last year. Grand-mother fed the whole thing to the dogs, and Amalie had again signed several declarations that nobody wanted to remember, even she couldn't remember, and the dogs got more and more bold and greedy, once they attacked Grandmother when she left the house to visit the Sig-norina of the Society for the Prevention of Cruelty to Animals. That was tragic, said Grandmother, and since Father laughed when she told the story because he was having a good day, just promoted to Director of the Board of Health, which put us all in a good mood, she said to him: You stupid boy.

It is rare for Father to listen to Grandmother's stories. They are all intricate and entangled like life itself. No beginning and no end. Meandering, always losing the thread. Grandmother doesn't want to leave out anything essential that comes along, and at the end she sits there and asks us if we remember what she wanted to tell us.

When we used to go on Sunday family outings because the car was new and a novelty, then Grandmother sat up front, Mother and I in the back, I holding tight to Mother because Father drove faster and faster as Grandmother told story after story, sometimes he even drove into ditches, then Grandmother was very quiet for a few minutes. And when Father had forgotten that she was sitting next to him she remembered a story, and so it went every Sunday until everybody else had a car and went on outings. Then we stayed home.

Dear Hermine, Amalie writes, thanks for sympathy card and black socks and tea. You forgot Band-Aids, and centaury and pocket knife for the cheeseman. Asked again about you. Roberto had a son. Greetings from Amalie in the hot South.

Every letter ends like this. Let you know with great pain that my husband died fatally yesterday. Don't laugh, says Grandmother. She's a poor soul and can hardly see anything. She never learned German properly in the Steiermark because she was a simple woman, and she knows only the basics in Italian. Don't ever laugh at the simple people, said Grandmother. Close the little casket. Although I would have liked to know what was in the letters that Father wrote from the front where he was in charge of the hospital. We destroyed all those letters, says Grandmother.

I don't believe it. You can believe me, says Grandmother, I never lie. And Mein Kampf? Why did you keep Mein Kampf? It must have been dangerous to keep Mein Kampf when the Russians occupied our city! That is different, says Grandmother, I hid it in the attic, like everything that will be a collector's item one day. Our Mein Kampf is a first edition, after all.

When the Soviets liberated Czechoslovakia from Dubcek and Co. many people in our city grabbed Mein Kampf and hid the black books again in the attics. Grandmother got the Russian textbook from the attic and put it on the kitchen table. After all, her kitchen door is the first door when you come into the house, and if they come, Grandmother said at that time in August, I'll show them the book and say: Me no Fashista, me Catolica in Austria sempre. Because that sort of thing always helps, it also helped on the train between Rome and Naples, when the other travelers looked at her angrily and didn't want to give her room to sit and rest her suitcase. So Grandmother pulled the big gold crucifix from under her blouse and said: Io mamma dottore in Austria, io Catolica sempre.[5] Then the Italian who had a knife on him jumped up immediately, put Grandmother's suitcase into the crowded corridor and even offered her the window seat.

She would also show the golden crucifix when she is

5. Translation of her pidgin Italian: I'm the mother of a doctor in Austria, I've always been Catholic.

short of cash in Sicily and is hitchhiking to run a few er-
rands for Amalie. So she never gets raped, and Father
was always happy that Grandmother behaved that way
only in Sicily. Until he found out that even at home she
sometimes hitchhikes from one farm to the next to get
fresh bacon and eggs. A patient who had once picked
Grandmother up talked about it in the doctor's office.
Madame, your mother, he said. That caused a big blow-
up. Once at Christmas Grandmother had a black eye and
bruises on her face. She had been in an accident, but
never told us exactly how she got into that car. The man
who had picked her up was a proletarian, and Grandmother evaded all the questions. Then Father found out
that sometimes or in fact almost daily Grandmother
asked the patients in the waiting room who among them
was the last in line. When the last patient came forward Grandmother sent him to the butcher's. Once
Father was finished a little early, and the last patient
came running up the stairs out of breath. He explained
his mysterious disappearance, and Father had to see
him, although his office hours were actually over.
Father threatened Grandmother that he would abandon
his profession if she couldn't finally learn how she
should behave as the mother of a doctor. I know that
better than you do, she said, you are simply not a
practical person.

Are you keeping a diary? Rolf smiled. Why didn't you tell
me you wanted that sort of thing? I'll buy you a real diary, with keys, then you can lock up your little secrets
and hide them from me. Do you really have any secrets?

No? Has anything happened? What do you write in your diary when nothing has happened?

Please read it.

No, you should have your privacy, God forbid.

He brings me his desk lamp so that I will not ruin my eyes, he fastens it down, but cannot find the extension cord. We must look for it. We find it under the dirty laundry in the basket. He forgives me, sets the new light up on the table, connects it, asks why I look at him like that and if I mind that he is lending me his light. Don't stay up too late, it's already past midnight! He comes out of the bedroom again, his portable radio under his arm, sits down behind me, waits, is wearing his light blue pajamas again. I have taken off the little pocket. What are you thinking about? Maybe you can't think of anything more today because you're tired? Why don't you come to bed?

Shall I stop?

No, I'll get a book for myself. I'll read while you write. I find it touching to see how you sit there and look as if you are thinking about something important. He utters a sigh of relief when I close the notebook. Scolds me because I am about to tear it up. We turn over the pages. It is from my elementary school years. Local History. At that time my handwriting was round. Not mine. I used to admire Gerlinde, whose handwriting flowed so nicely, and I simply copied it. Later I admired a girl with a tight angular handwriting. So I gave my handwriting an angular look. Then I wrote like Father. To this day I have kept many handwritings. I can change my handwriting at will, and perhaps my own handwriting is not even among the many I use. That happens, says Rolf, because you do relate to the people living around you after all. Why the insistence? Now he admits that his mother has complained about my lack of contact with the world around me. I go to the bathroom, Rolf follows me, and I relate to the toothpaste, the toothbrush, the moisturizing cream, the brimstone, have a deep relationship with my nailbrush, my deodorant spray that is now on the bathroom shelf, motionless like all the other little friends in the bathroom, and a moment ago they were all chuckling about me. There was a man in a movie who simply swept his hand over the crowded shelves of the woman who caused him grief, and he swept everything onto the bathroom floor and stared with satisfaction at the cosmetics all flowing together. And at the broken glass too. I do only useful things. I brush my teeth and use the toilet, Rolf is waiting, I comb my hair and squeeze out the pimple that bothers him, I cannot make noises, the neighbors are sleeping. Rolf says the bottles in the American movie contained only dyed fluids. I shrivel to a bitter seed that wants to spit itself out. I will write that into my housekeeping book tomorrow.

Why do I have a bad conscience when I visit Karl? The house where he lives with his parents looks shabby. Kitchen smells meet you at the front door, from somewhere you can hear the grunting noises of his sister who was born healthy but whose meningitis went unnoticed. Deaf and dumb, she walks around in the kitchen with stubborn steps, her hands folded over her chest, growling, putting her head on the shoulder of Karl's mother, wanting to be caressed, and Karl's mother asks if she can still call me by my first name while she caresses the head of her thirty-year-old daughter, saying that her little girl is so affectionate and needs so much love.

Karl is upstairs, says his mother, he'll be happy to see you. But Karl does not answer my knock at the door. When he is drunk he usually takes two sleeping pills to remove himself for a while. I did not come to ask him what moonfish breasts look like. I wanted to know what he meant when he said once: Probably you are for me what the moon is for Caligula. Karl has read Sartre and Camus. I kept all the letters he wrote to me. I was proud that someone wrote me letters that were so smart that I did not understand them. Probably I was knocking much too softly. Yes, Karl works a lot, perhaps he got tired and lay down, says his mother when I say goodbye. Say hello to your husband, she shouts after me.

My mother-in-law is knitting, she always knits with her chin pushed forward. Her regularly shaped dentures, new from Linz, are impersonal. She puts all those little light gray teeth in a glass of water overnight. When she talks I am always afraid that her smile might suddenly fall out. She wants me to call her Mama. Often I am speechless with fear when she smiles at me like that. How would I look if everything fell out and only a hole were left? Where would I look? She used to be an accountant. Even then she had that shrill insistent voice so that you were sorry the moment you asked her anything. My mother tells me this, she used to take her tax problems to her. My mother-in-law likes to give advice that she packages in threats. Every problem you want her to shed a ray of light on is quickly darkened by wild allusions to everything that could happen to you. People say that Rolf's father used to have his wife sit in his office when he was unable to get rid of a customer.

She spreads butter and sugar on toast because Rolf told her that I have a sweet tooth. Don't worry about the pimples, you will lose those after you have been married for a few years and you have children. It's all right, eat. She is knitting something gray. Her husband was also small and gray. He had high blood pressure and had to be careful with seasonings. At dinner when her back was turned he quickly put a lot of salt on his meat. At night he slept in the living room because there he could put his feet up. Because of his illness. People say. Mother-in-law knits everything into her gray wool. She says: You should knit. She wants to sublet a room to a nice student, but of course there are no nice young girls anymore. Anyway, there are no female students here, Rolf told her. She is indignant: Whoever goes to high school is a student. And she would like to sublet in order not to be alone. Rolf is against that because it does not look good when his mother sublets. My husband used to make noises while eating, she says, and he liked to listen to marching music. Listen, you do like me, don't you, she asks, what is your size, I will knit a nice sweater for you. Rolf will not believe his eyes!

I remember my father-in-law's funeral. We were having Latin class. Our Latin teacher went to the window and let us all look out of the window. The funeral procession came right past our high school and there I saw little Rolfi walking up front, with his mother. He was the most important person in the whole funeral party because he was the only son and because his father lived on through him. And it was so sad that now he had only his mother left. Perhaps I married him because of that? I remember a night in May, Rolf was already quite tall, suddenly much taller than before, beneath the window, and he had rested his bicycle against the fountain on the main plaza, and he and Albert and Karl, and others of his class, they ran around the fountain. Why? Anyway, Hilde was standing next to me, and she pointed to Albert, and then I pointed to Rolf, that was like an agreement. At that time I did not know that Albert had a birthmark on his chin. Albert did not have anything at all. Neither did Karl. Rolf already had the bicycle, and he let me sit on the bar once. My mother was very angry at that, but my father smiled with some satisfaction, and I thought: Now I am in love. Mama was just knitting a nice day of her marriage into her wool. It was on Mount Postling, and she was carrying Rolf under her heart, and below them was Linz, it was after the war, and her husband confessed to her that she was the first woman with whom he had anything at all. Me too, I say, I have had only Rolf and no man before him. You see, she says, that's very rare.

The Latin teacher is still there. I see him on the main plaza, he addresses me with deep respect and shows me a little note that he always carries around with him. He has marked on it all the warnings and failing grades he has given this last school year. He says I should compare that with all the warnings and failing grades his colleagues have given. Those are also on his note, and one can see that he is not the harshest but only the second harshest. I do not know if he is happy or angry about that. Perhaps he is carrying around that note only to get through the long summer vacation. There is a rumor that he has lung cancer, and they want to force him to retire. But he will not retire because those who graduate from universities these days are not really qualified to teach. These days almost anyone is admitted to study at the university. Even workers, if they pass a special exam. Can you imagine, he says, going to a doctor who used to be a worker and has taken that special exam, and you are supposed to undress in front of someone like that? The Latin teacher is wearing leather knickers and a ruby red jacket with silver buttons. And why should I have lung cancer, when I haven't even smoked for decades? He says that Rolf was always his best student. And Madam, you yourself have known ever since high school that you were not born for academic life. He kisses my hand, and I wish him a speedy retirement.

Look what I brought for you!

I don't want a dog.

Of course, it is quite natural. Rolf wants to please me by buying himself a setter, and I protest against having an animal in an apartment without a yard. I thought you love animals, he says. Precisely because I do love animals. But now he has already bought him, it is as simple as that: goes out and buys one because he wants something alive and because his wife has so far not told him that she is expecting, and we are petting the brown spotted fur, we make up across these sharp little teeth and the rosy tongue, across these suspicious eyes beneath dog's wrinkles, this animal is purebred, you can tell from his palate, from his price too, and Rolf wants to train him well, and I may give him a name. Laurence? Laurence won't do, it must begin with a *B*. Blitz? How did you think of Blitz? There was a dog who had a mistress, but no real home, and one day Blitz was found shot in the forest, and his mistress was annoyed that they did not at least bring her the corpse right away as long as they had killed the dog which had been her property. She would have liked to make a bedside rug of it. So we name him Blitz and make amends for all that. But please don't spoil him, says Rolf, and even if you aren't happy about it, at least buy him some meat every other day. That's not asking too much, is it? But I am happy! Are you really happy? Yes!

Blitz whines when Rolf approaches him with the leash, one, two, three, he must be punished. It is imperative to set this creature straight until he is housebroken. Otherwise he'll ruin our floor. Don't you understand that he has to obey? We can't have it any other way. You can't argue with a dog, you know! But you don't understand that. Rolf did not really expect me to understand his training methods. I am supposed to leave that to him. And the dog is stupid enough to lick Rolf's hand after his punishment! He is getting meek. Wags promptly and patiently, knocks over a glass when he is careless enough to express his joy next to the coffee table, immediately gets hit on the nose for that, yes, he has to learn his lesson, what are we going to do with a dog that constantly damages things? And I tell you for the hundredth time: Don't let him run around the apartment freely when you are busy! Don't tell me again that the dog needs a yard. Can't you think of anything else?

Blitz has his official residence in the visitors' bathroom. He is allowed to sleep on an old car blanket. He is to wait, his leash fastened to a hook on the wall. He is happy when someone comes home. We can hear his tail hitting the wall from all the way down the stairwell. If he lies quietly and does not tug on the leash he is untied as a reward. But he can only leave the bathroom after Rolf has given the command. And when Rolf unties him and forgets to say the word then the dog sits there and waits. Lifts his head, lowers it, listens carefully, after a while lies down again. Until his existence is remembered. Then he shoots out, jumps up on his master, is reprimanded kindly, and, come on, don't be sentimental. A dog does not have the range of feelings of human beings. What are canary birds in their cages supposed to say? They don't say anything. See?

Blitz is afraid of cars. Small and stubborn, he sits at the wall of the house and trembles. He is also afraid of the man who sweeps the streets. As much as I pull on the leash and make it seem harmless, he resists, doesn't want to go, just sits there and trembles. Even though the directions say that his breed runs thirty kilometers every day. Besides, he hasn't barked once yet. Maybe he is not a real dog at all? He has a bladder infection and an inflammation of the middle ear, but Rolf says he will make a dog of him, I am not to worry. To your place, Blitz! Blitz races into the visitors' bathroom. Come back! He dashes around the corner and is sitting here again. To your place! He races around the corner. Come! Quickly back again. Rolf notices that Blitz is cheating. He doesn't dash anymore to the bathroom when he is ordered to his place, he just races behind the corner and waits there because he knows that he will be ordered to come right back. We are both proud of the intelligence of our child, and yet Rolf has to employ his teaching device because consistency is everything.

My husband throws out words, and they fall where he wants them. My words are weightless. They hover around the room blocking the view. I can catch them all again. Do you listen when I talk to you? asks Rolf. Yes. What are you thinking about? About what you say. What did I say? That I shouldn't be a disgrace to you tonight. And? That I should be nice to Albert and Hilde. And? And just chat normally. What else? That I am not wearing the bracelet you gave me and that you are sorry to have given me your grandfather's silver pencil holder because I negligently misplaced or lost it. Come on, says Rolf, let me kiss you. He caresses and praises me, don't be so stiff, give me a real kiss, unbutton your blouse, look me in the eyes. I can see the white circles, but there was a time when I loved those eyes, and I am keeping a photo where Rolf is sitting in an armchair in my parents' living room, he is laughing, I used to like his nose so much, his shirt pulled to one side, I used to like his cuff links. A real man, I thought, and when I was in doubt whether I still loved him I got out that photo and knew: yes, that's the one I love. Kiss me! He didn't used to say that so roughly, I probably did it voluntarily then. I imagine us playing a scene in a movie. That has always helped. When I had done something wrong and had to account for it to my parents and show remorse, I used to think that I was a child star playing a role. Cut, twenty-seventh take: Woman kisses man. He unbuttons his permanent press shirt, throws it on the floor, suddenly behaves like a bachelor, and I can only think that I have to wash it. But he doesn't care about the shirt now, and the skin on the inside of my thighs is sensitive. What he's doing is desecration of a corpse. I am still thinking that afterwards I have to wash and iron that shirt.

Afterwards, he winds his watch. That's one of his habits, to turn the screw, his thumb is broad, he holds the watch to his ear, listens to how time, time, time ticks away. One day has twenty-four, one hour sixty, times sixty, times sixty, eighty-six thousand four hundred seconds tick away every day. How many days have we been married? He is not afraid that something could run away from us.

What should I be afraid of?

Don't you sometimes think that you could go blind in

one eye and then you'll think: How much that eye let me see!

You can still see halfway with one eye.

Or that you will die?

Everybody has to.

What comes to mind when you are thinking of dying?

My life insurance. That's what you want to hear, isn't it? You just want it confirmed over and over that I'm the fool you think I am?

When Karl was still writing stories I read in one of them: And now this kiss tasted of nothing but flesh. There was a time when Rolf's and my kisses didn't taste of flesh. We asked ourselves if we acquire a kiss by kissing. Whether every person has an unlimited or a limited number of kisses. We would discuss that while we were kissing each other. When I still unbuttoned his buttons and he mine. When I was still allowed to interrupt his kisses without him asking: What's the matter? Why are you so stiff? Your theory of the finite number of kisses is right, he once said. Because if you were always just kissing you would starve. And so we gave each other a very long kiss.

Something happens while we are eating, something is pulsing in me, a ringing begins, and Rolf puts the fish bones on the edge of his plate, Hilde explains antiauthoritarian education to us, Albert is silent, and there is a kiss for him in my mouth. Hilde says she doesn't care that the teacher criticizes her son's bad handwriting. Sooner or later she will buy a typewriter for her son. Albert raises his glass and looks at me, but he doesn't drink. Hilde nudges him in his side: you say something. Albert agrees with her. Hilde wants Rolf to admit that what he just said about antiauthoritarian education is wrong. Rolf says he found with his dog that authoritarian education and so on, until Hilde is offended. She rejects such comparisons. Albert asks me about my horoscope. My children are difficult, says Hilde. She claims: You don't have children, so let someone who knows tell you all about it. I ask Albert about his horoscope. Hilde asks why we don't have children. Rolf answers elegantly. I smile to Albert that I don't want children by Rolf. He smiles back that at this moment he also would rather not have any children by Hilde. Rolf and Hilde ruffle each other's feathers without messing up their hairdos. It is an argument pro forma. If a woman wants to prove that she is not stupid then you give her the opportunity, as long as she is not the one to whom you are married. Hilde demands that Albert admit what she just stressed. Albert admits everything. Hilde says he has come around at last. I think that so far I have given much too little thought to horoscopes. Maybe there is something to it. We all nod our heads when Hilde declares that only children make a woman a true woman. Rolf voices a minor reservation, but he lets Hilde win. Hilde as our guest is queen. A successful evening. I haven't been a disgrace to Rolf. When Hilde and Albert are gone he helps me clear the table and assigns plus and minus points. Plus: I was pretty. Minus: A little too quiet. Plus: You let Hilde speak freely. Minus: But you didn't talk to Albert at all.

Minus: Hilde dresses better than you do. Minus: Why don't we have children? Rolf is tipsy, he wants to make love to me, the meal was so heavy after all, that's not a criticism, that's a motive, and he is almost never wrong, but here he is always wrong, he says: it hasn't been so good with you for a long time. And all that while I wasn't even home.

Where are you going? Walking? In this weather? Yes, I know you love the rain, but that's no reason to catch a cold. Yes, I know you're taking an umbrella, but don't you want to tell me why you must go for a walk while it is pouring? At least leave the dog at home!

Rolf is right. Blitz doesn't have an umbrella. Our dog also gives off too strong a dog odor when he lies under the heater soaked through and through. So I'll leave Blitz at home. But he's already sitting in the entry hall because I made a familiar noise with the key. He's waiting. He too likes the rain. Wait, says Rolf, when it's dry we'll go for a walk together.

Blitz and I are waiting in the entry hall. Rolf is getting dressed, the rain has stopped, the lights are hanging in the haze on the avenue, we meet Albert and Hilde, what a coincidence that Hilde is accompanying Albert, after all she has such difficult children. Hilde says Albert suddenly had the crazy idea to go for a walk in the rain. Blitz gets bored with such conversations, he runs ahead, jumps up on the chestnut trees to stay fit for forbidden cat chases, and the four of us are walking slowly along the avenue with two big umbrellas.

Blitz is waiting with me, it's taking so long, Rome wasn't built in a day, Grandmother has always known that, she would say that now too, if I could tell her what I want, the first stirrings of my own will in many months. I keep it to myself, only Blitz gets it whispered in his ears, he sighs full of understanding and is discreet. At night when I desert the marriage bed, softly, not to wake Rolf, Blitz comes trotting quietly, not to wake Rolf, from the visitors' bathroom. He protects me on my tours through the dark rooms. We grope our way through the kitchen to the kitchen balcony. Concrete walls. You cannot see the other wives who are perhaps also standing on their balconies now wishing to jump or fly, and when I stand at the railing too long the dog lies down at my feet and when I grope my way back he trots around his corner back to the car blanket. He isn't angry and doesn't make a fuss about his loneliness. I put my face in his nice fur and ask him how he can stand it. Blitz sighs. I am waiting. You learn a lot from animals.

How Rolf tells the joke about the man who comes to Vienna and says: Snow on Kilimanjaro! And the one about the man on the train who sits across from an elegant woman. And the one about the man who goes to Hell and can choose between two possibilities. And the political jokes. And another political one which is so old already that probably no one knows it any more. And how the audience forces itself to laugh and then everybody quickly tells a joke so that the situation doesn't become embarrassing since there wasn't much laughter just now, and how all of that doesn't bother me anymore.

What are you doing? What kind of a dance is that supposed to be? That's not a dance! And without music? How am I supposed to understand that you have the music inside you? Watch it, you're falling, explain that to me about the music! Have you been drinking? You're in a good mood, just like that? Why don't you say so right away? May I share your cheerfulness if for once you are cheerful? Wait, I'll put on a record.

We haven't danced with each other for a long time, Rolf and I. He is looking for the turntable cover, where is it, of course it isn't where it's supposed to be, but no matter, and left two-three, now we'll practice the waltz to the left, be patient, you'll learn it eventually, you have to dance it with me at the next Association ball, lean your head back, be graceful, be supple, why are you so clumsy, now it's better, one, two, three, not such long steps, don't step on the dog's paws, don't be so tense, your arm, your arm, not so hard, be pliable, yes, that's good, Blitz, to your place, the dog is jealous, just look at that, Blitz!

Albert's car coincidentally stands at the fork in the road where Blitz runs fifteen kilometers twice every day. It's a gray car. Albert is wearing a gray suit. He has smoked several cigarettes. The stubs are near his front tire. He is really waiting quite by coincidence. Asks if he may accompany me a little. Yes, do, but it will be a long walk. Albert also likes long walks.

He went the whole way through the forest with me. And back. With a rest. Fir needles, moss strands, pine needles, fern. Since when? Since that evening. It was a successful evening. Yes, it was a beautiful evening, you were so quiet, you too were silent, do we want to be quiet all the time, yes, we do. From now on he'll accompany me more often. Extended walks. Blitz will have to wait alone, below the fork in the road, tied to a fence. It's his fate. Rolf has prepared him. When the whole car disappears then around the curve I untie Blitz, he sits on his hind paws, look, I am still here, bend down, let me lick your chin. He is not allowed to lick. Rolf has forbidden it because dogs have worms and the eggs of the worms have barbs, but I bend down, and the dog licks, my body feels like lead when Albert is gone. People in cars are fast. Humbly, Blitz and I trot home.

Where were you? With Karl, I say. I don't like that, says Rolf. Why not? Because Karl is no company for us.

I am standing at the edge of the forest when there is a wind from the Alpine thaw and the snow flows to slush, and the gray car comes, I get in, we drive into the forest. I wait at the edge of the forest when the fields are dry, then the gray car, Albert gets out, and we walk. It is even possible in the doctor's office whenever Albert is scheduled for house calls. Then he spreads a white sheepskin in front of the fireplace, Hilde bought it in Greece, two cushions from the waiting room, we have a bottle of vodka and two little glasses, cigarettes, the cigarette lighter and the ashtray from the waiting room. We kiss each other very long. With Rolf I've forgotten how I enjoy un-

dressing someone. I feel young, so naked, and decent because I feel young again. But Albert doesn't have too
much time. Come on. But I am here. And do I like his
body, yes, yes, I should say so without his asking, yes, I
like to feel you, and how do you like it best, I don't know,
maybe I like everything best with you, I like your big
tummy, Albert, don't be fresh, no, really, I adore your
tummy. There must be women who like tummy, nature
takes care of that, since after every war there are more
male than female babies born, and when men get fat
women begin to like tummies, and Rolf is much too
skinny, in addition he has wire under his skin, from his
spleen operation, you can feel it, okay, it's not his fault,
actually I used to always like him very much for his wire,
but he does knee-bends every night and makes his toes
go around in circles. Don't talk about Rolf, Albert says.
We'll talk about nobody, nobody, not even about us, wait
some more, yes, I am waiting, stupid, I do want you to
come, do you love me? Albert doesn't answer. I think, you
don't ask that sort of thing in such a configuration. I am
quiet and let his big moan break over me and rain down
on me in little splinters, and then we are lying exhausted on our Greek island, each of us banished into ourselves. Tomorrow again? Yes, tomorrow again.

You were with Karl? What do you talk about? Does he
read poems to you? No, we talk about social politics.
What sort of views does our Karl actually have? Diffuse
ones. You can't expect anything else from an alcoholic,
Rolf says and hugs me as if in conspiracy.

Sometimes I go to Karl's too. Right now he is quite busy with his principal, who runs a special education class at the school although there aren't enough special education students, and so he simply declared some children to be half-idiots since such a special education class is more lucrative, and nevertheless Karl's principal can sometimes be found at the school for an hour at the most because he is so busy as a hunter, fisherman and landowner. Members of the Board of Education have a hunting license in the district of Karl's principal, so the school inspector overlooks these things, and in a different school in a different town it is the other way round, says Karl, there they declare children that need special education ready for regular classes in order not to upset the parents. At that school there is a principal who has the students work in his nursery during off-school hours, for ten shillings an hour. Karl filed a complaint against him, but the proceedings were dropped without calling witnesses. The teachers who knew about it reproached Karl with uncollegial behavior. And under such circumstances I am supposed to write my little poems? Karl reads a lot, and sometimes he finds a sentence in a thick book that he marks. He wants to make this one sentence into a book since everything said around that sentence is superfluous. But then, says Karl, I dissolve two sleeping pills in beer and drink myself to a state of dizziness that throws me on the bed, hoping every time that perhaps this time my circulation won't manage it.

I am a well with a lot of water, Karl says. The cover has to be broken in. Will it be worthwhile? Perhaps the water is foul? He will write again only when the business with the lid has been solved somehow. I think, you can also lift off well covers. You only need the proper tools. Karl has so many notebooks with material. Some day he should organize everything and squeeze it into chapters. But it always swells out from between your fingers, when you touch life, he says, it's like mercury. Mercury is fun, but it is also poisonous, and the cheerful novels that some writers force themselves to write, some of them die of it. He takes notes because life becomes bearable for him if he can describe parts of it now and then. Because he arrives at more precise feelings and thoughts while noting things down. He believes that people can be reached better in writing than in speaking. When reading they pay more attention and they are less vain.

Mother is happy that I have a good marriage. She says that my father doesn't understand her. Grandmother says that she went through a lot with Grandfather. Father says that Grandmother never understood Grandfather. Grandmother says that Father should respect Mother more. Father says that Mother doesn't understand him.

I just have to imagine that they are not Rolf's handkerchiefs but Albert's, that I brush the sofa so that Albert isn't bothered by dog hair, and I stretch the sheet over the marriage bed as if it were our island, I fold the pajamas as if I were Hilde. Maybe Albert folds his own pajamas? Does he sleep on the right or the left side? Hilde uses Oil of Olay. She has smaller ears than I and more delicate joints. Rolf thinks that recently I have been smelling better and looking more well-groomed. He cannot fail to notice that with time he might make a true woman of me.

You have been getting more sensible, Father says, one can talk to you now. You used to be like stirred-up sand in stormy water. Now the water is clear. The sand is set- tling. Father pours us some cognac and offers me one of his black cigarettes because this is an adult now who sits across from him. And he says a lot more, while listening to himself attentively at the same time. One can't talk to your father, you know, says Mother, but you are the new generation, she says, and when I look at you. Well, what do you think? She says that she is thinking what she might have thought in those days when she was pregnant if she could have seen me then as I am sitting in front of her now. But secretly she collects unhappi- ness, she clips it from newspapers and pastes charred children's corpses, drowned horses, maltreated cats into a calendar with sayings for each new month, also dried wildflowers, doves' feathers, landscapes painted by hand and by foot, and in her nightstand she has tucked in Ta- gore, Rilke, Hesse, and Trakl, and bows and giftwrap, letters all of which she keeps while Father tears up every letter that has been read and answered, and in the drawer of his nightstand there is a leather case with in- vestment papers, and on the lower shelf are his slippers.

Your father is materialistic!

Your mother lives in castles in the air!

Your husband is a character, says Grandmother.

Rolf is, of course, not jealous of a moron like Karl, how could I think that of him, but I should please be considerate, don't tell Karl things that concern only the two of us, he hopes that I have enough tact not to step over the line between openness and shamelessness, and where is the button, it has been missing for weeks! That's what you get when you constantly smooch around with the damned dog, you probably need your own husband for nothing more than to warm your bed! He doesn't wait for the answer. Leaves without slamming the door. If only he would slam a door once! But he controls himself, he probably learned that from his mama and the military, he has himself under control, and people like Rolf give a kick in the ass with a conciliatory smile. In this way you cheat business partners and show nasty salesmen out the door. Inconspicuously, but effectively, you brush off people. Brush off. He said that himself about himself and his boss, in particular his boss impresses him, I should see him, he said once into the darkness before falling asleep, when again there hadn't been anything, with one stroke of the pen he makes heads roll! He leaves and continues to think for me, even means well, only thinks past me by a hair's breadth, and he doesn't know where his own good begins to turn rotten. He has no eyes in the back of his head, looks always ahead, and marches on.

I ask my mother if it ever happens that a person you pictured in a particular way could suddenly change or if the image was wrong, or if you yourself change. I don't change, she says, your father has changed some. I think men change. Only men? Yes, she says, and then something that once hurt occurs to her. Not Father, but someone whom she nursed during the war when she was still a nurse in the hospital, she took the most serious cases voluntarily, she still has corns on her feet because the shoes she got were too small, and they didn't have bigger ones during the war, so she stayed up many nights in her tight shoes, and she got the dying people out of their death chambers, and there was one who wrote her these idealistic letters later on. But when his injuries had healed he sent her Christmas greetings with annual reports about turbulence and major events, about motorcycles that his working wife sent to the U.S. while he sat in his administrative tower and wracked his brain over organizational improvements and cost-cutting activities, and he used to send her volumes of poetry with one of his own poems inserted in each. And now he was chasing petty criminals and whizzed around at BMW, reported on the production capacities of Opel, VW, and Ford, and they had to endure the drought, and that he himself was still driving his old Fiat, and that his wife had to have her affected kidney attached higher again because it had dropped and that she was feeling very well, and that for twenty German marks per consultation every three months even the diverticula in his intestines were quiet, and in the garden he had lilac and forsythias, and he was paying three hundred and fifty

German marks a month, garage included. He is one who did change, says Mother, but perhaps his wife made him that way. She never signs the letters. Perhaps that's why? There was another one in the war whom Mother saved, and he wanted to marry her, but he misspelled catarrh, and my father found that impossible and said he would draw her upwards to him, and they got engaged on the afternoon of the morning when Mother fainted during a leg amputation, then Father definitely fell in love with the nurse with the ruined feet. When Mother believes herself unobserved the corners of her mouth droop. She believes I didn't listen. It's the wine's fault that she talked so much and cried a little. Grandmother says, unfounded sadness comes often, but with age contentment comes too, since old people don't have any more wishes, and you have all the unwished things behind you.

But when Albert really does go on house calls since he can't let people die because of me, though he could, for all I care he could, then I lie down on the bed, leave the window open a crack, and the noise of the street comes like slumber rumbling, each car that passes is gray, rays of sun stream through the curtains, you lose consciousness, slip into a suction as into death, not afraid anymore, then the phone rings, Mother-in-law is going to Linz for shopping and wants to know if I need anything. I come along, on the bus there are schoolchildren who give off a strange smell that we used to give off as schoolchildren. How good it was to be a schoolchild and not to know how dangerously we lived, and in Linz I buy black underwear to give my life some meaning again. The saleswoman claims to own one of every item I try on, and she may as well see: Albert has branded my shoulders with his marks. I belong to him. My breasts have enlarged under his lips. His experience, his orders, my obedience, his: Let yourself go! Just let yourself go for once! He determines when the right moment has to be. Yet it never comes because I'm always thinking about it and because Rolf has made a mess of me. As far as Rolf is concerned, all women are normal except for me. Albert says there are no normal women, only stupid men, and that arousal happens automatically, exactly when you are not thinking about it it happens, and that for a woman it is beautiful even without a climax. He loves my cheerfulness. I buy everything that is black. The saleswoman thinks that she's done it again. My cheerfulness arises from looking forward to Albert's cheerfulness. Blitz is allowed to run under the prison wall in the city park although it's forbidden. We'll lift all bans. People get vulture and turkey faces from observing too many prohibitions. I write a letter to Albert: Let's stop the lies! Don't handle the steering wheel and me at the same time when we drive in the car! But the letter cannot be sent off. I wade in crumpled sentences because Albert loves my reserve.

There are several ways to go. One leads out of town on the western side, past the Cafe Lichtenauer and across the town's moat bridge. There used to be a tower, you can still see the curves in the foundation. At some point the tower burned down. If you cross the street that goes around it you reach a parking lot. A giant parking lot for a few cars. This street was built when they thought they could count on tourism because our small town is on the Czechoslovakian border, and you could suddenly feel again that we were border country, there was traffic into and out of the Czekei, as we say here. An autobahn was supposed to be built. Our merchants were counting on higher sales. Then they closed the border up there again, and only the detour street is left. It goes past the monastery of the Brothers of St. Mary. The walkway forks off here. I can walk up the shriveled sand path to St. Peter, past gardens and villas, or around the cloister walls I can reach the area "behind the Marianum," where there are small garden plots, single-family homes, meadows, a playing field, old folks' benches. Here I know every stone and every tuft of grass, here I meet the same people again and again, voices, gestures, here Karl grabbed me and tried to kiss me one winter night. Rape me, I thought, but he apologized and also wrote a letter to apologize a second time. Here someone whose name was Rolfi pushed his damp hand into my low-cut dress, and there wasn't anything there yet, I had faked it with Kleenex, and because I pushed away the thirteen-year-old hand, Rolfi thought of me as virtuous. That could have been it. Behind the monastery of the Brothers of St. Mary are those who are dying out one by one, and we don't know their names when we hear: That one has died now too, and she did not survive her pneumonia. But you get help, and then everybody knows: the man with the yellow cane, his hands were always trembling so much, the woman with the plaid scarf on her head, she had a shaggy dog.

There is another way around the town, out through the Linzer Gate, then right across the avenue, past the brewery, to the Lichtenauer Bridge, to the ice skating rink where they play tennis. Ever since the ice skating rink which is not used in the summer has been covered with red soil, you know who belongs to the better circles in our town. We, of course, are among them, Rolf and Albert and Hilde and I. Past the tennis court along the rusty iron bars of the fence around the town moat, the ancient, hunchbacked, stooped houses, their slanted tiny windows, and the pond full of carp that snatch up pieces of bread tossed at them, past the convent of the school nuns, where I was taught that the Jews murdered Jesus and how to crochet a potholder, and that a girl isn't allowed to whistle because with every whistle that comes from female lips the sweet Virgin Mary weeps one tear. Across the street you get to the other avenue, the gloomy one, along the creek, more walls of iron bars to imprison deer and reindeer for all to see, please don't feed, the pair of deer are called Karl and Hilde, past the mill whose owner died of flour dust in his lungs, past the city walls where the prison and rectory sit side by side, everything behind walls. But the prison is no more. There are no real criminals in our town. And if there are they are taken to Linz. The last one was while the border to Czechoslovakia was open: A German had driven through the no-man's-land without stopping. He was questioned by the

Austrian border patrol, he showed his papers that were all in order, but just for the sake of order he had to spend a few days in our prison because he just kept saying: "It was just for fun!" They didn't know what to do with that, and it was summer, the roses under the prison wall had dark blossoms, and in the evenings many people went into the city park to see the madman's face, but he didn't show himself, they were disappointed, and it turned out that he really had wanted to drive from Czechoslovakia through no-man's-land to Austria without stopping just for fun.

There is also the walk to the edge of the forest, and Albert has been waiting there since 5 o'clock, now it is seven, he was afraid I wouldn't come anymore, he imagined how it would be if I didn't come anymore, felt unhappy, felt like choking, and then, says Albert, you came walking up the path as you have never walked before, and the clouds separated, the sun came out in order to see you running up here, and a crow started singing, yes, you know, the crow simply had to sing when it saw you.

More, much more would have to happen, and we don't say anything because we are afraid of the lie or of the truth. We love each other without loving each other, look for each other without looking, we are content with crumbs, and are you cold? Yes, I am cold. Oh, my poor you, he rubs my hands, I love you, love you, oh you, oh you, my mouth is dry, let me drink from your mouth, come, and on the way home the air gets so dark.

Albert asked me what my sign was, and they claim in the

Taurus book I bought to find out more about Albert that the marked Taurus type can be easily recognized by his gait. He gives the impression of having all the time in the world and of knowing no hurry. He stands firmly on the ground and follows the law of gravity better than anyone else. According to the book Taurus, physiologically speaking, has a connection with the sign of Scorpio, which dominates the sexual and excretive organs. About the Aries woman it says that she knows outbursts of passion which she wants to satisfy on the spot. Infidelity is the sword of Damocles hovering over her marriage. Not much is needed for her to abandon her home, shatter her marriage, and get a divorce. Natural good-naturedness makes the Taurus a henpecked husband in extreme cases. Is Albert an extreme case? Every time he talks about Hilde, he says: My Lovely. And the book says that the Taurus is unshakeable in calling his wife his better half. I gave Albert the two books, but he said, what would his Lovely think if he came home with books, suddenly, when she wants him to read Simone de Beauvoir and Alice Schwarzer, and he just skims through the books because in the evening he is too tired for anything, even for reading.

A little something for you, says Hilde's single neighbor and puts a glass plate with cake and apple tarts in Hilde's kitchen after her Sunday baking, and these little somethings are always dusted with powdered sugar. When the neighbor is gone Hilde leaves the plate standing around someplace. The neighbor is dirty, and nobody wants her cakes, and so the little somethings dry out and fall apart and land in the plastic bag of the garbage pail, and when on Monday the neighbor comes to pick up the plate she asks how it was, and Hilde thanks her, the neighbor leaves and is happy, and soon she comes again, with nut crescents and vanilla cookies, dusted with powdered sugar, and through the years such little somethings pile up like dust to dust because, after all, Hilde cannot tell the neighbor that everybody recoils from her.

What else do I know about Hilde? That she has to call Albert repeatedly before he comes to dinner. That she wonders why he suddenly doesn't like her Mexican roast anymore. Since he used to love her spicy hot food. That now he could certainly use her hot food, she teases him, and since he begins to eat without a word she really believes now that he is cheating on her, and she wants to know from him whether what she suspects is true. Whether he thinks that she doesn't notice anything? He doesn't seem to hear that, and again: Hey, you, do you think I'm stupid? And then she tells him things that only people who are married to each other will say. That she bears everything because of the children. Albert also bears it because of the children. One day the children will bear it because of their own children and perhaps with the same words will now and then shoot off little arrows that are not supposed to destroy anything, only hurt.

Laughter and the clinking of glasses in the respectable restaurant. Once Karl was forbidden to come on the premises, because he stood up and shouted over to the table of the regular customers: Nazi pigs. But that was exaggerated. Not all of them were national socialists, and those at that table, they used to believe in their cause, there are no pigs among us. Wood-paneled walls like in Grandfather's coffeehouse, when suddenly there were many glaring lights around the billiard table, sit down at the piano, but I can't play piano, that doesn't matter, sit down and put your little fingers on the white keys, rectangular patterns on the tablecloths, the owner of the inn himself serves us, that's an honor. He pushes the cork in a little before he pulls it out. He has done that hundreds, thousands of times, and he does it better and better. People sing a song, Hilde has to go out, she doesn't say where, she says: I must go somewhere. I move closer to Albert, let my hand glide under the table, his hand glides after it, our fingers with their rings link together, we hug each other with our hands, we squeeze each other's air out with the palms of our hands, squash our crippled love flat, and Hilde comes back, we move away from each other, Hilde puts her purse on the table, pushes herself between us, I again next to Rolf, she with Albert, we may, must, want to sit like that, in the car, at home, with her he falls asleep, she is with him when he wipes the sleep from his eyes in the morning, she can see him when he takes a shower, and perhaps Albert flattens out the toothpaste tube also and rolls it up, scolds Hilde when there is a piece of soap left lying in the water again, does he smoke at home? Does he laugh when his children say funny things? Do you mark her with your lips? Do you coo when Hilde pulls her fingernails over your back too? Do you smile like you do with me? Or perhaps Hilde cannot stand your smile anymore and the clearing of your throat that is the beginning of your lie? Perhaps she hears you clearing your throat even when you slam the gray car door shut and cross the street towards the house, just like I can see Rolf's tightly squeezed lips even before he comes up the stairs, when he opens the mailbox downstairs, he brings so many letters into the apartment, and there is never one from you to me, you never picked a flower for me, and you buy some for her, and perhaps she wants you to stick the gladiolas up your ass because you only bring the flowers and nothing else.

And Father gives Mother security, Rolf gives it to me, Albert gives Hilde security, and Rolf discusses with Albert the problematic aspects of Japanese tuna fish, which you can't eat at all anymore because of the lead content, and Hilde explains to me the wonderful effects of a sauna twice a week and how her child kicked for the first time, and Rolf could tell Albert something really important, and Albert Rolf, and I announce that I'll open the Chivas now, and Albert confesses that he has been waiting for nothing else the whole time, and Rolf forbids me to talk about the price of the whisky, and Hilde is fighting with me about opening the expensive bottle, she snatches the Chivas away from me, Albert reprimands her: Don't make such a fuss. But she isn't making a fuss. She is really fighting, but not against the whisky, and Hilde doesn't even want to know why my plants have dried out, and I don't want to talk at all about the disadvantages of central heating, nor about whether I have a green thumb or not, but to make it easier we agree that

I don't and Hilde does, then it is quiet. We can't get anything out of the Japanese fish anymore, Rolf crosses his
right leg over his left to break through the silence, he
swings through it with his one foot, and Hilde quickly
places an old subject of conversation on the table. We
pretend that it is new, but even our ears are worn out.
We can sleep ourselves away with open eyes. Alcohol
thickens the blood, everything they say now I hear
through a jelly wall, and then Hilde after going to the
bathroom wants to know where I bought the towels, how
much they were, and everybody quickly adds everything that comes to mind about towels.

Of course it is shit, says Karl, but you went over to their
side, now you have to stick it out. Those are common-
place stories that you're telling me, don't bore me with
them. Rolf is jealous of me? With every woman I thought
of you, says Karl, I believe I loved you, and I was unfair
to those I carried on with since it wasn't their fault I
didn't want to have you and destroy you. Do you know
what I do when I am worn out with work? I get drunk,
write a poem, write a parody of it right away and a parody on myself, then the pills, and every evening the same
anesthesia, and in the morning I get into my VW, drive
to school, tell the children some lies about history and
German composition, everybody believes that I believe
what I say, and when I come home I look forward to my
sister's clumsy touching and think that she lives in
peace.

Work takes over the senses. You are not at the mercy of

the temptation to think about the sense of your work. So much is to be done! There is always a drawer to be straightened up. On Sundays Mother picks sweaters, belts, and underwear, purses and blouses from the closet, then she puts everything back in place. You cannot disturb her in this. It startles her when you address her in a loud voice because she is really engrossed in her organizing. Who knows what she really takes out, puts aside and places back. In any case it calms, and Rolf is a calm person because he is an orderly person. He wipes off the dust from his shoes before he enters the entry hall, takes the dog leash from a hook and hangs it on the correct one, hangs his coat on its hook, washes his hands thoroughly, checks if the mirror is covered with little white specks again. No, today the mirror is shining bright. The woman did the cleaning. She is standing at the bathroom door, he sees his wife in the mirror, goes to the bedroom, takes off his shoes, sits on the bed, puts the shoes down where they belong, takes off his coat, sees his wife at the bedroom door, what is it with her, why is she watching him today? He loosens the button under his tie. How I envy him at this moment, that he has a tie which he can simply pull over his head. How he is he and not I. He finds a hair clip on the rug and puts it on my nightstand without any reproach. If he would only bring on a little nausea in me now I would vomit words.

We are the nails, Karl wrote once, with which God builds his house. The house must be firm, and every blow must hit the nail on its head. We hold out our heads, and each blow hurts, but after all we are the nails. God is dead, Karl wrote to me in another letter. Who's supposed to know what to think?

Rolf figures how much money we make. He says we. What we earned this year and what we will earn next year, and in the twentieth year of his employment with VOEST, how much he will have earned for us by then. I am not supposed to pull the threads from the tablecloth when he discusses the future with me. And why am I sad, since he loves me, he wants us to be in harmony, and he didn't want to strike Blitz, he just shot a charge of slugs at him to stop him from hunting chickens. It is normal for a hunter to shoot past his dog with slugs to shock him. But Blitz turned around, a slug caught his eye, and now it is swelling, discolored, but Blitz was driven to the vet hospital immediately, got anesthetic, he surely didn't feel anything, he just reared up and in his deep sleep jumped off the operation table, whined on the rubber floor, and the vet said it was better not to operate, the empty eye socket would ooze constantly. If the animal should have headaches you can mix tablets into his food. Or you can put him to sleep. Rolf says that the dog was too expensive for that. And I am not supposed to be hysterical, Blitz doesn't know that he is blind, you know.

He doesn't know it, he just bumps into table corners, knocks over objects, doesn't see the cars coming from the right, he howls, barks, rubs his eye on upholstered chairs and everything soft, rubs his head on the coats of people who visit us, and sometimes he rubs his whole body on people. He is too much of a nuisance now. The neighbors complain of the noises that come from the apartment at night. Rolf doesn't want enemies because of an animal. It is better for Blitz too, he says, and then everyone has to make sacrifices. Blitz belongs to Rolf. Come, shake hands, good, car, come, look how happy he still is when he hears car, it is really a shame, Rolf says. Blitz runs ahead, down the stairs, bumps into walls, sits down in front of the car as he has learned, waiting and tilting his head while Rolf unlocks it, jumps on the back seat as he has always done, licks over the leather because he is not allowed to lick Rolf's neck. It is his last ride. The chewed-up rubber ball remains. The car blanket with hair. The leash.

Must the whole town hear you? You don't even cry like that for a human being! You can't be crying for that dog, there must be something else. Finally Rolf strikes, but what I have doesn't give. It sticks some place and grows, the skin yields, it hardens because it wants to grow more, and it doesn't have enough room, pushes into the toes and fingers, and my clothes are getting too tight, and so is my skin, and I want to take everything off and shed everything off myself. There are moments when I feel an urge to grab glasses so that they break, to crush and break everything and to run away, but where, and I suppress all that as long as the skin stretches. Without skin you would be lost. Without skin no one could look at you. Unbearable if someone were to burst and suddenly be without skin. You would be able to see everything. How often have I said everything and not known what I was saying.

On Sundays the air gets so viscous that birds get stuck in midflight. The river stagnates under the bridge. Sunday belongs to people who live in well-regulated circumstances. On Sundays I am allowed to drive the car since I did get a driver's license at the same time I graduated from high school. Graduation and driver's license, my father said, are like writing and reading. Rolf gives advice so that I can manage in traffic without having experience of my own, then I have to let him have the wheel again because he is getting nervous, he feels sorry for the car, the clutch always groans after my driving. Why aren't you talking? he asks. He says you can look at the scenery and still say a word now and then. I light his cigarettes and give him the other glasses, the ones from the glove compartment. And when he brakes we come to a stop, and when he steps on the gas we drive ahead. What do I have against normality? Some cars that are coming towards us are driven by women. I feel in the swirling air how the men are watching them.

When I walk across the fields without Blitz I think that I won't be defeated by the grotesque faces that force themselves on me. I visit the cemetery and read all the names and am not afraid of newly dug graves since the earth is open to take us in again, and here a wind that will clothe us grows, and anyway we already carry the skull under our hair.

Sundays with music, but please, not that caterwauling. Paganini doesn't caterwaul! Well then, de gustibus non est, what is it again? Don't you remember? Cave canem! Say what it is, says Rolf, I want to know if you've really forgotten everything. There is no arguing about tastes. No, in Latin. He imprints on my memory: disputandum. This Sunday Rolf knows an unusual number of Latin phrases, and the street under the window is hard, I would just have to bend out a little further, I am only a heartbeat away from the pavement. I loathed Vergil, says Rolf, but I enjoyed Tacitus.

Grandmother sits safe on the kitchen chair, her knees wrapped in warm compresses. Nothing really can happen to her anymore. Her dress buttoned up to the neck above her breast that has fulfilled all its duties. She has always been a decent girl, everybody liked her, she was hard-working and friendly, and Grandfather took her because she was suitable for his business, and before the wedding Grandmother wrote a letter to her aunt with a request for the facts of life. Her aunt explained to her how it is, and gave her the advice: if that young fireman is a decent man and owns something, then go ahead right away. She has never been sorry, and Albert doesn't want to jeopardize his marriage, you don't get a divorce just like that. Why is he caressing me while he is saying that? You can't live without some lies. Did he say that or did I think that? Now Albert is talking like Rolf. Father, Mother, why didn't you prepare me for this? Why did you conceal so much from me? Why does he hit at me with words and lie naked next to me and talk about his wife with whom he is trying to find an inner bond again, why does he tell me that, how do you grow a scab so that nobody can step into open wounds anymore, how do you prevent wounds from happening? Get up, get dressed, empty the ashtray, cover up the traces. Why is he kissing my eyebrows, if only he would squeeze tight and strangle my thoughts. You understand, Albert says, and that's not a question, that means: That's how it is!

Melancholy comes softly, it sneaks in with the poison that makes you sick but doesn't kill. Rolf is sitting there hunched over his hands as if they were going to pull him down. Ever since I've confessed it to him he has been roaming through the rooms at night, talking to himself, looking for something in the liquor cabinet with which to wash away thoughts. Thoughts cannot be outwitted. Nor drowned. They come back when they find land again. Dig their tracks into the sand again. Thoughts are crabs. Obtrusive. Resist you when you try to resist them. Come back in different shapes. There are thoughts you have to come to terms with, you have to get used to in order to survive them.

Albert is embarrassed that I had a weak moment and told Rolf. Asks if I think that Rolf will tell Hilde. How would I know that? How did he react? What did he say about me? He must have said something! No, Rolf was silent about Albert.

I too have habits. The habit of standing in front of the mirror and thinking that I will scream and that the mirror will break to pieces from my scream. I have the habit of taking a book, opening it, closing it, putting it back, for it is only a book, nothing happens in a book because the pages are already numbered. I have the habit of

standing between the curtain and the window and looking at the room, to see how it looks without me. Rolf has
good razor blades. Go to the sink, put your arm in it, then
he'll come home and find his wife half in the sink and half
down the drain. Grandmother would fall off the kitchen
chair! Father at a loss. Mother would suffer for it and
take all the blame on herself because it is easier, such an
agreeable burden without contours, such vague guilt
feelings are easier to bear, but please no details, the
whole weight all at once, that'll weigh less, that's why
my mother always takes the whole blame upon herself
when there is something. However, one doesn't kill oneself. And even if you are deaf and crippled, leprous, if you
are a burden to everyone, if you are caught in an insane
asylum and you have to be cleaned up three times a day,
one doesn't kill oneself. I have the habit of taking Valium. With it you dream better and merely have fur on
your tongue in the morning. But you can wash that away.
Rolf says, he read some place that half of all women are
addicted to Valium. But they didn't explain why. I asked
Rolf, Rolf says I should ask Albert. And why Albert gives
me Valium while he positively prohibits Hilde from taking it. Perhaps to get rid of one of us? You are crazy, says
Rolf, and I can see that he is feeling better. Now a lot is
clear. Wasn't your grandfather, the gambler, schizo-
phrenic? And your father, doesn't he like to drink, at
night?

Who is Rolf supposed to swap vacation stories with? For
that too you get married, so there is someone you can
share memories with. In any case he wants me to ac-

company him. Who wouldn't want to go to Majorca? Albert and Hilde took a plane to Greece. You always have to travel in the summer. On the plane Rolf explains how the jets work and about the air pressure in the cabin and outside, and the food, that it is frozen and thawed, or doesn't this interest you? He is flirting with the stewardess, although she is just a flying waitress. At least that's what he told me when I wanted to go to flight school because I couldn't think of anything else to do. He asks the stewardess all those things that he knows anyway. He shows me on the map where we are flying. And why a plane flies. Oh, I see? Does this bore you? Anyone who sits down on a plane should at least know how all that works, how it takes off and lands. Fine, so he will stop explaining things. He leans back. Space is tight on planes. I can't move without bumping into Rolf. And the stewardess comes as a flying saleswoman, but I don't want duty-free perfume, so he buys one for his mother.

Rolf has a stomachache and diarrhea again. Barely on foreign soil and his organism fights back. The unusual food. In the Siesta Mar Hotel the water is too soft because it doesn't have enough calcium. You notice it when the soap can't be washed off easily. He explains. I understand. Finally. Palm trees, cypresses, cacti, lemon bushes. Rosemary grows in the mountains. Rolf describes his digestive trouble while we are having breakfast. And how often he had to go to the bathroom during the night, how badly the toilet flushes, how backward people are here, how poor people are, how primitive, how greedily they grab the tips.

White boats on the horizon, purple sunset, the wind

carries a lot of dust through the twisted little streets of the old city of Palma, our milk in Austria has more fat content, there is better service at our gas stations, our buses don't have these antediluvian exhaust pipes, our streets have more intelligent signs, and how do all the cripples get here? Spain wasn't in our war. Oh I see. They had their own. Girls with cloth shoes, when they laugh they really laugh. Children wrestling for sunflower seeds. The blue bay at Deya, the cemetery up high, people used to live to over a hundred here, the youngest dead person is sixty-eight, what could he have died of? We drink almond milk, men are sitting on the rocks and fishing, the water comes and goes and comes and goes, the pigeons are flying without colliding, and on the plane Rolf studies the security measures again, doesn't flirt with a stewardess because he feels dirty and tired after this vacation, since all we did was argue again, and he really did wear shorts and a peaked cap! I was ashamed and was ashamed for being ashamed. And for his not noticing anything and for having chosen Rolf among all possibilities.

Karl has fallen in love and has gone to an alcohol treatment center voluntarily. Mother doesn't know anything more, just: the girl has an illegitimate child, is employed by a bank, also has a vw, her parents are against Karl, and she made an agreement with Karl. If Karl comes back and doesn't drink for two years they'll get married. His mother is very happy. His sisters and brothers had wanted to force him to give up alcohol before. Because when he was very drunk he often said he would light a fire and burn himself and everything he had written. Because he wasn't getting anywhere as a writer anyway, and that had always been his dream. His mother has loaded potatoes on a little wagon. It is the baby buggy that they sat in one after the other. Karl and his sisters and brothers. At one time. In those days when I watched at lunch how Father drew a design into the tablecloth with his fork while he was waiting for the food. It had to be that way. The napkin and the fork and the waiting were there so that Father would draw designs. There was a thick vein on Father's temple because fathers have to have veins on their temples. Especially when they chew.

I am returning to the apartment in which Rolf and I chew and draw designs. Step by step, don't rush, don't cry, be putty in Albert's hand and crumble when he throws it away, he returned from Greece so brown, I would like to know if his whole body is so brown. Call Hilde and ask? On the outskirts of the city old women sit on colorfully painted wood benches that were donated to our little town by the beautification society. On each bench it says on a metal plate who gave it. The wife of the chairman of the beautification society is supposedly also addicted to Valium. When she greets you in an especially friendly way she is at the peak of its effect. Albert's car passes the avenue. He is on a round of house calls. My father is also very busy when he returns from his vacation. My father took care of Albert's patients during his vacation.

Albert greets me inconspicuously. He just raises his arm from the open car window. Rolf says, I shouldn't get any ideas. After all, Albert has a lot of female patients. Mother says when those females see a white coat they immediately get romantic. And many have themselves examined more often than necessary. And one of them still had the price tag on her new little panties when she undressed in front of Father.

A phase of silence. It crumbles off, and the sand runs, the only audible thing. We say good morning to each other and dinner is ready. The meat has coarse fibers, where did you get it? Next door. Where were you yesterday? With Albert. I can't forbid you, says Rolf. Yes, I know. And if I ask you not to see Albert anymore? What would you gain from it if I didn't see Albert anymore? No, we don't say anything. We only say good morning and dinner is ready. The meat is okay.

Albert separates my hollowed hands with a blow. He doesn't want me to drink the water from the pond in which we went swimming. Last warmth of fall. The soft thing I stepped on was a rabbit cadaver. Albert says, you get typhoid from such water. What is typhoid compared to you, Hilde, and Rolf! Silly girl. Yes, I am so silly. I will never understand your rules. And in the winter there is a gloomy period, perhaps I'll kill myself. Don't be childish. Be nice to Rolf. Let's make the best of it. Will you call me later today? At five he calls from his office. He says that he is just eating a sausage sandwich with a green pepper. He bites into it in my ear, I hear it crunching, and that of course he loves me, otherwise he wouldn't have started anything with me. That now he has to hang up because a patient is coming. Gall bladder colic. And wonders if he should prescribe those vitamins again for me. Be careful with the Valium. Take it only when the tingling under the skin of your skull gets to be too much. Of course, love has to do with hormones. And everything, even the loftiest feeling, can be traced back to the sexual instinct. And that every person is lonely to a certain extent. That he has to hang up now, not because of the telephone bill but because the gall bladder colic just rang the bell.

Every year in the fall there is a celebration of a friendship that we women cannot understand. You find that some men can only feel really happy in herds. There they sit and have lost their hair and acquired phrases and fat, and children. The wives compare lipsticks and perfumes in the bathroom. From the other side you can hear laughter. What do men laugh about while they urinate? No woman will ever know. Hilde has been drinking too much, now she feels badly, she bends over the toilet bowl, wants to go home. Her expressionless eyes! She is shaking with chills while I am driving her home in Rolf's car, put my arm around her, like Albert would put his arm around my freezing body when he didn't know what to say. It's already light. Tissues from Rolf's glove compartment for Hilde. She wants to have a good cry, not especially with me, but now she does anyway after she has said that I made a fool of my husband, that I am a little whore, broke up her marriage, that she has known for a long time. I am a human being, she says, not an animal in a cage that you only feed and marvel at, why doesn't he confide in me, why does he think of me as less understanding than I am? I am used to that with him, he sticks his prick in everywhere. Excuse me! Hilde is frightened and cries, and she does love him, he and she belong together, why did he have two children with her and place her on such a high pedestal that she can't get down, he raised everything so high up. Sometimes I would like to jump down, but in my dreams there is always only water, I always dream of water, says Hilde, and I could climb the walls when he doesn't come home, and there used to be times when he would come home late at night, when all that concerned me was that something might have happened to him.

What was it like? Hilde looks at me with amazement. You don't know what that sort of thing is like? Doesn't your husband ever come home late? No, Rolf is punctual. During the first years it always happened the same way, says Hilde, I am lying there waiting and waiting, and then he comes and says, he knows that he is a bad person, and I say: Nonsense, and he embraces me, and I am thankful that he embraces me and is nice to me, and he says that he loves me and then he snores. That's how it went. And now? Now I know that he is a cowardly swine, and if I could I would kick him. Rolf's tissues are not enough. She blows her nose in my Italian silk handkerchief, thanks me for taking her home and says I should forget what she had blubbered about, it's not all that bad, occasionally you lose your cool, it's just the drinking.

Sunday walk, Albert's little son is throwing chestnuts, Albert's little daughter is crying, are you also a mother, the boy asks in the restaurant gardens. No. Then why are you having coffee? He hides behind an elm tree and wants us to look for him. We don't look for him. He comes and spits on Hilde's new dress. Hilde scolds him and promises him a toy for Monday if he'll be good. I don't want any more toys, says Albert's son. He has a birthmark on his chin. I report that Karl wrote me a letter from the alcoholism treatment center. He wrote that before his commitment he felt like a living dead man, his friends had slowly and quietly left him, occasionally he fell in love with a girl, but it was never love, and he had always wanted to write a real love story, but could only stare at the typewriter and at the books that could tell him nothing anymore. Albert's son gets an authoritative spanking because during my story he spit several times on Hilde's dress. So she must have listened. But now she just sighs, and Albert and Rolf talk about TV antennas.

When I wasn't alone with Rolf and Albert yet, when Blitz was one pet and I was the other, when Blitz contracted his eyes and looked like a Chinese, then I spoke Chinese to him fluently and Italian, and in all languages. I performed my plays for Blitz, and when Rolf came home, I continued performing: I opened my arms, let Rolf's tired noble head sink on my shoulders. For Rolf never had an ordinary head, always a noble head. Blitz didn't applaud when I acted for Rolf. He saw through the game and saw an objective in it. What's wrong? asked Rolf, in the beginning still curious because some of my inanities were capable of making him laugh. So, what's wrong? I think, what's wrong is that I need a meaning for my life. Astonished glances from Rolf and Blitz: Isn't that what we are? Responsibility is what I need, an interest. But you aren't interested in anything! That may change. Do you think so? Yes. When I tell you about my job, said Rolf, you yawn through your nostrils. Because I don't understand your shit job! What? Rolf, do you actually understand your job? Of course. Well then, what do you do all day? For God's sake, he thought, she asks such idiotic questions again. Do you understand VOEST, Rolf? Of course. As your wife could I identify with your work? Yes, you could. Do you identify with your work? Yes, I do. Darn it, he thought, I just want to eat. Do I contribute to your work at VOEST by taking care of your physical wellbeing? But of course, my sweet! And how about the nation? Of course, my darling. Does VOEST supply steel for weapons to Africa? How did you get that idea, my sweetheart? He says that I have too much imagination. I refuse to cook noodle soup for someone, who in a company, in which steel, with which weapons, and so forth, in short, I don't want to kill people with my noodle soup. Rolf thinks that this has to be the most farfetched excuse ever for a wife who doesn't like household work.

Perhaps he is right. But what he said about my imagination reminds me of Father. When I reminded him of a childhood observation, when I would say: Father, that time when you said this or that to some man. Oh Lord, this child has an imagination, he said then. Rolf asks if maybe I have my period. No, I haven't had a period for a long time. Are you pregnant? I am nothing at all. I am only I, and you wanted me, and now you have me and see what you have, and when you realize it then I don't suit you. I wanted a normal wife, Rolf says. Why doesn't he employ a housekeeper? Why doesn't this machine treat himself to a whore? Does he know how much he would owe me if I were a whore? Rolf says if I were one then I would have to learn a lot. What, for example? To be obedient, for example. Every whore has her pimp. But I would work as a free-lance whore. And who would protect you? Blitz. There are Seeing Eye dogs, watch dogs, why shouldn't there be whore dogs?

This was a stimulating turn of the conversation, and the noodle soup was so rich in calories. Then Rolf unbuttoned his waistband, after all I've become a passable cook since I have been pledged by sacrament to occupy myself with material things, and now I want to be a whore on top of it, what more could he need, and he did legalize what he wants, so did I, I don't have to wait out in the cold and snow in the streets, I have my steady customer, for him it's cheaper, and that's the security he gives me. Then he helped clear the table, he always has an ulterior motive when he lends a hand, and that time he rewarded a special service, and later he became suspicious, thought for a long time while he sat there and didn't say anything, asked what I read and do all the time when I'm alone at home, whether I live a double life in thoughts or deeds, and I said: What are you thinking of. Of course my imagination actually did bring Albert to our bedroom when he had too many patients, and the fantasies of a housewife can become dangerous for the household. A wife is to cultivate no imagination but her husband's, and if the husband doesn't have any because he rejects imagination and fantasies, then morally I am not entitled to indulge my imagination alone. Besides: She said whore. But you talk like a man, said Rolf.

You are not pregnant?

The doctor looks at the nurse. Sterile, hard-working team. The nurse puts tubes into an American machine that came across the ocean for leukemia patients. Leukemia is incurable, but here you can flush out the many white blood cells temporarily. Say to death: This is General Hospital, please wait! So I don't give up yet and say good-bye to the world. Incidentally, Ferdinand Raimund committed suicide just like Kleist, like Tucholsky, the latter with poison, however, and Adalbert Stifter with a razor blade, and my great-grandfather with a rope, even if Grandmother denies it. She said, he didn't really want to hang himself, he just tried it or pretended it to frighten the others, and he was tipsy, then he fell into the noose, slipped, cried out for help, but nobody heard him, it was night, and he was tipsy every night. This machine costs more than a million shillings, the government pays for it, every cleaning of a patient costs seven hundred because they have to throw away all the tubes afterwards. The nurse explains that to me very precisely because I am the wife of an educated man and will understand it.

I don't think that you are insane, says the doctor, merely melancholic. When the machine doesn't function, he means the motor of life, my gall bladder and my liver where my sicknesses originate, then that has an effect on the mood. So he takes a blood test. The nurse takes a sample. She has a round, strong chin, wears earrings, smells fresh and seems very happy with everything: with the doctor who is her husband or lover, with the machine that connects her with people and the man. They work together. That's it. I believe the nurse and her doctor understand each other well. Free yourself, the doctor says.[6] He means: take off your dress and everything else. Does this hurt? No. And there? Not there either. And now, does it hurt here? No, that feels good. He blushes! You don't say that when he pleasantly touches pleasant parts of the body merely for medical reasons. Nevertheless it feels good, and I would like to cry because he makes everything so pleasant and asks nothing besides: Childhood diseases? That's easy. Jaundice, measles, German measles, middle ear infection. I had everything, appendix and tonsils removed. Once I

6. This odd expression from the German has been retained to avoid losing the sense of the passage. The German *Machen Sie sich frei* (free yourself), meaning get undressed, operates as a pun in the larger context.

was in love with my husband. Removed. He kissed me for the first time when I was ten, he sixteen, my cheek got quite wet, he was pushing his bicycle home, I was carrying my first kiss home, stood on a chair, Frieda's soaked stockings were floating in the sink under the mirror, I examined my first kiss in the mirror. Frieda was allowed to know everything because she was my nurse-maid and explained the facts of life to me. But Mother disputed that children come from where Frieda claimed they came from, and my mother slapped me on the cheek and broke the kiss because you don't go catching may bugs with some Rolfi, if there are no may bugs this year, and because this Rolfi's mother had called at home, worried, and perhaps I loved him up to the time of the wedding because they broke that kiss without warning me. The doctor puts a blood pressure cuff around my arm tenderly. The nurse watches without jealousy. After all, I am only a case. I could cry. But this is only measuring blood pressure and my blood pressure is quite normal.

But as an insane person you wouldn't know that you are insane, the doctor says. Do you mean me? No, just in general, insane people don't know that they are insane. Your husband as an engineer doesn't have the right to make a diagnosis, the nurse says. I'm just an internist, the doctor says, even I would never make a diagnosis that doesn't fall into my specialty. Maybe you are pregnant. The nurse fills several glass tubes with my blood. Suddenly she puts her finger to her lips: I am not to speak of suicide, now the patient with leukemia has arrived. The doctor draws a curtain between the woman and me. I just saw that she had a brownish-blue face. Couldn't we trade places, she and I? We might help each other out. Cover yourself. Get dressed. Why am I not crazy? If they only knew how my head roars. I would like to hold it under a circular saw to stop the noise in there.

Why do you want so badly to be insane, the doctor asks. Do you smoke? The nurse hears that he is about to light a cigarette and passes an ashtray through the curtain. I am afraid that I may be, and it is the belief that gives you the feeling of being crazy even if you aren't, and so forth. Are you never afraid? The internist shakes his head. No weariness of life? No, definitely not. After all he has this nice job and the nurse. Those two have so much. He doesn't think he is crazy. Then perhaps you are insane because you believe that you are normal? He laughs: it's not that simple. Oh yes, I believe life is very simple. But we shy away from simplicity, we put ornaments all over it and hide in them, and whoever doesn't want the ornaments has simplicity, but that makes one inept for life.

And? And I can't go on. I wrote that into my housekeeping book when rice got more expensive. My husband used to like to read my housekeeping book because that way he had me under control, in every respect. But now I don't make entries anymore because I have a relationship with another man. So that's why you definitely don't want to be pregnant, but insane, the internist says. How can I convince him that I am sick? Recently my husband has also been quite worried because every day I say the opposite of what I said the preceding day.

But that evens out every three days then, the internist says, and you have only two opinions. No, it's always a new opposite! Then you are changeable, and that's no problem. But he doesn't like me to be changeable. Who? My husband! He had forgotten my husband completely. Because he is already thinking of the next patient, the one whose blood will be washed there behind the curtain.

Even Beethoven's nephew wanted to kill himself. Because my uncle tormented me so, he says. Beethoven was a miser and he controlled his housekeeper. Secretly he went to the marketplace and counted how many spoonfuls of sugar his cook put in the coffee and whether that balanced with his calculations. Beethoven and Rolf, the great savers. The internist tells me he'll notify me of the results of the blood tests. Then the nurse runs after me, into the hallway where all the people are sick, they have it good, and she says she'll call me as soon as there is any report or write to me, I don't need to come back. Those who are sitting here in the hallway, they are corpses, but they're still warm.

Why doesn't anybody believe that I am sick? Is it healthy that every month I wait impatiently for the bellyache so that my child may be spared, that I think *saved* for all my unborn children, each month, and that I would really rather be dead than alive? Those are crises, says Albert, but just wait till you have a child, you'll see how you'll change: You'll have responsibility and material that is alive. And I? Then you will think of your child and no longer of yourself. The hospital doorman doesn't look at me at all, the way I walk so healthily past his station. He isn't curious about healthy people who go to the hospital. Aren't caretakers ever curious just for the sake of curiosity? Rolf said: female caretakers are curious. Sometimes you are like a caretaker. Because I wanted to know who was pacing back and forth in the apartment above us during the night. Who up there also wasn't able to sleep. That's none of your business, said Rolf, don't be curious like a caretaker. Do I have gas, the internist wanted to know. Yes, no. What did he mean? Do I have bellyaches. No, not exactly. But my heart. And the nausea every morning when I wake up. My heart hurts all the way up to my arm. From smoking? Else you are pregnant, he said. When we get the results or in the meantime if you get your period, then everything will be clear. Clear. He really said that. *Clear.* And the woman behind the curtain doesn't know that she has to die. They don't tell her because it wouldn't make any sense to tell her. She believes she is almost healthy again.

Please think, says Rolf. Analyze yourself. I remember the lemon-yellow dress, again and again, and I can't think about anything else. What was the whole thing really about at the time? You cling to details, he would say, so I pretend to think, but I think about the dress. You bear a grudge, he would say. Yes, I do. I bear everything, I collect all the rocks that he jumps over and bear them, and it can't really be the lemon-yellow dress. It seems you are brooding. Dissatisfied that you don't have a job? He says: I told you, if you want to work, then work. And what about that experience with the tax consultant? You went to his office, didn't even finish typing the letter, in the middle of the dictation you jumped up like a crazy person and declared you didn't want to work after all. Who is supposed to take you seriously? If necessary I can be convinced that numbers don't interest you. But that numbers depress you, that you break out in a cold sweat at the sight of numbers just because you must type them without being able to envision anything? You don't have to be able to envision something all the time! As office help you just help the office, that's it! And in a tax consultant's office you type the letters, damn it, which the tax consultant dictates! He knows his stuff, don't worry. And whether you like or dislike the people you address with Dear Sir, whether you love them or not, that's enough to drive you mad, type the letters and that's it! If everyone thought like you do, no thanks! Yes, just get drunk. But don't buy this bad liquor. Since we have connections at the Atomic Energy Commission. If I call in Vienna, I can do that from VOEST and it won't cost me a penny, my friend Walter will get us liquor from the duty-free shop. I see, you don't want to get drunk through the auspices of the Atomic Energy Commission. What actually do you want? Perhaps you will provide me with a list so I can know where I am and so I'm less confused about you.

What do I want, he asks, but he doesn't really ask it. He says he hates arguments and that I always start arguments. Especially when I've been drinking. But the conflict is growing closer, and the discord has gotten to

102

be like a disquieting tune that won't go away. Always the same thing. He wants to expand my freedom and buy me a used car so that I have more of a free rein. My maliciousness: I don't want a used car, I would rather go by scooter, like we used to. His harmless test: Show me where the shoe trees are. Here, my beloved, are your shoe trees. Now take them and put them into these shoes. Why? Don't ask, put them in. I obey. You never know, perhaps the biggest joke of our marriage is coming, everything was just a dream, now we'll laugh and everything will be fine. Rolf isn't laughing although the shoe trees are already in place. He says he always suspected that. What? His shoes have gotten deformed because I always put the shoe trees in the wrong way, that is, the left one into the right shoe and the right one into the left shoe, and now they bulge everywhere. I am sorry again, Rolf calls me his good child, I say it is brutal what he did, this test, and everything else, he says he will never be brutal again, nor sadistic, tomorrow everything will be different, don't take everything so seriously all the time, he has his special sense of humor, and I always put everything on the line.

But why doesn't the tax consultant type his own letters? Can't he type? And why wasn't I allowed to wear the lemon-yellow dress on Friday? But that was more than a year ago, that rag, Rolf screams. Rag, he said, after a whole year he still says rag. So then, why wasn't I allowed to wear that lemon-yellow dress a year ago, on that Friday? Because you look childish in it. He doesn't like it, feels provoked when I wear it. That I love it: fine.

But the fact that I still love it when he hates it proves that I don't love him. The dress has become an issue of power.

Rolf bought two new lemon-yellow dresses. And I insist on the old one. Then he says: please show some consideration for me. Everybody says you dress ridiculously and they can't understand why I don't buy you better clothes. So when you wear that sweet little dress you give people the impression that I am an egotist. Besides, everybody, even Hilde and Albert, everybody says they don't understand why you don't pay more attention to your appearance. We are closed in by gossips and gripers, Rolf! The only person who doesn't always have a ready answer and who asks you real questions is me! But those are disquieting tunes.

Use your makeup with more care, shout more quietly, and anyway it isn't true that our life is monotonous. There are diversions: Monday, Tuesday, Wednesday, Thursday, Friday, and Saturday. Sunday. And Monday: a sales representative from Ried was here, Tuesday: four people from Graz, Wednesday: the English university professor. Thursday: Rolf helped his secretary into her coat. Although that is not company policy. If he had any say in the matter he would help her into her coat every evening. But his boss, the one who makes heads roll, is against it. On that Thursday night, however, Rolf helped the secretary into her coat because he had a half-private, half-business talk with her after work. And so he would have been embarrassed to stand next to her, without doing anything, while she was putting on her coat. So he helped her into it and made an exception for the first time. But now he doesn't know what to do. He cannot be the only person in the company to help his secretary into her coat. How should he have behaved? I think he did the right thing. He thinks so too. We understand each other. I think he should help her into her coat if he and she both feel okay about it. He said he understands my point of view, and he shares it, but that would be rocking the boat.

What shall I do with the note? It says that I will deliver in seven months. Enough iron and vitamins to give birth to a healthy child. The internist did say: You are strong. A child with a birthmark? On my walk with Albert I choke a wish even before it is quite spoken. Half-sentences are dropping from his mouth. He pushes his lower lip forward like a little red spoon with which he dispenses medicine in small doses and precise numbers of drops. An egg is no chicken, and the egg must go. If Albert says so. And how he says it. How Albert's face suddenly changed over the note with the happy news. It is shrinking by the minute, and his body is growing and growing, his eyebrows are becoming antennas. Albert runs his hands through his hair jerkily and over and over again. Such a thicket above such a small face. Why didn't you take the pill? Because I was relying on something impossible. Is it really impossible? Albert talks about blackmail. To prove that I am not a blackmailer I go with him immediately. To his office. Curtains shut. Lie down on the table. Clench your teeth. Spread your legs, relax,

relax completely, slide down further, it's no big deal.

I no longer understand anything. Am I oversensitive because I feel humiliated? That he comes with that big iron hook. How often has he just as quickly taken care of that sort of thing? He apologizes that he has to do it without anesthesia. But you did get two injections. That little pain is only the spasm. The uterus has to open, you see? I have a uterus. Now that it is being robbed it really strikes me for the first time that I have one. Albert is scraping skillfully. He does it with those same hands that he put on my thighs yesterday and the day before yesterday. Then they felt so good. Those hands. He has always had those hands with him, from the beginning. Get down, we are finished. I put on panties, hose, shoes, and dress and cannot quite believe it yet. That's how fast it goes. If I should ever have a child it will never be my first. That one is in a pail. A glassy little lump, a few drops of blood on cellulose.

Up all those steps, there is a lift, but it has a door, and I can no longer open doors, just press one button, and when the door opens I just shout for help. This kind of person must be used to people just falling into his office and shouting something. But I say hello when the man stands in the door, such a little man with round glasses, how can he possibly help. He immediately entrenches himself behind a gigantic table. What can I do for you? Well, the man I love killed my child, I am married to a man I can't stand, he put my dog to sleep, and I don't want to live anymore because I can't stand myself anymore, the tingling under my skull, like bugs between the skull and the meninges, and in the mornings I wake up because my heart is quivering under a claw, during the day I would like most of all to lie somewhere under a rug, at night I have no more fervent wish than to fall asleep and never wake up again, and I sleep so deeply that it startles me when suddenly I am there again because my heart is quivering so, and I sweat, you see, I perspire, my father is a doctor, and he told me to always say perspiration and secretion instead of pus, please help me.

The little man says that I have the symptoms of a neuro-vegetative disorder. There is some medication, you take one pill after breakfast and one after lunch. Watch the alcohol. If that doesn't show any effect after a few days then you come back. That will be five hundred shillings. If you don't need a receipt I'll charge you only three hundred shillings. Next time and if you come regularly, perhaps for group therapy, it will cost relatively less. The little man gets up and accompanies me into another room. He shakes hands with me and squeezes my hand. He wants me to let go of his hand again. That's a rule, taking, letting go, all the things you do with your hands. He thanks me and pushes me out.

Railway stations, railway stations, people don't like them, humid and cold, sticky railway stations, with tracks that one doesn't cross because only those insured by the railway station may cross them, life, it is like that, my mother-in-law knits it into gray wool, all of life, life is a shorter or longer waiting period, interrupted by empty promises and bigger or smaller payments in cash, the conductor comes, he is only interested in my ticket, life is much too long for you to . . . life is short, my dear, one shouldn't take everything more seriously than it is, you take everything much too lightly, someone is reading a newspaper here. Somewhere the Turks are fighting against the Greeks, help the Greeks against the Turks, help the Lebanese against the Lebanese, suffered from depressions it says in the paper. A mother of four children bit an explosive to pieces in her mouth, foehn wave causes twenty-seven suicides, do something, finally you have to do something, hurt someone, but do something, find a religion, a party, read this good book, look out the window. The train passes cows, there will be cows every day although we eat their meat every day, the spider eats her mate after coitus, the human being is God's likeness, don't be afraid as long as there are human beings, you have to be afraid as long as there are human beings, how was it, asks Rolf who is punctual, standing on the platform. Expensive, I say. Yes, he knew it, that psychiatric treatment is expensive. How do you feel? Good. In my opinion you don't need a psychiatrist, says Rolf, but simply more will power. You let yourself go and you are much too sorry for yourself. Yes, I say, and the day after tomorrow is Sunday. The day after tomorrow we have to visit my mother, says Rolf. The day after tomorrow people will leave their houses to air themselves a little. In Sunday clothes. On Sundays those who normally walk stride. Everybody has their own way of moving about. You can tell every person from their gait. Rolf says I don't lift my feet. Albert always walks with his head stooped. Rolf goes in long strides. He passes and curses. Drive faster, you idiot. Yes, please drive fast, faster, perhaps something will melt in the speed of the flight, perhaps something will kill us together, or smash my skull when we are at home, as long as we can't talk to each other anyway, talk to the bugs, tell them they should stop, I've had my lesson, and I am speechless as you wished it, you did want to see what I would do when life deals me its first blow. The car has a defect, says Rolf, the windshield wipers make too much noise.

Mother doesn't want me to do that to them. What will it look like, the gossip in the small town, and have you thought that through. People enjoy others' misfortunes. Your father would be mortified. Rolf is part of the family, and there are difficulties in every marriage. To pay for a psychiatrist, that's not only a financial problem, but an unusual one too. You can't go to Vienna twice a week, you must see that. And if you got treatment in Linz, then it would soon leak out. Rolf is somebody in Linz. Besides, it costs money, and anyway psychiatrists are all nuts themselves.

Mother says I should not burden Father, and why don't we just have a child, Rolf and I, a child would distract you. My father is sitting in the living room poring over his maps. Every year when the summer threatens he draws in flight routes which he reads from the brochure Rolf gave him, even the ruler is from Rolf. Father imagines flights, Peking, Moscow, everything on the map and possible, purely a question of money. The dream is up for sale. I cannot really interrupt this dream and tell him that I need his help. Please, don't say anything, Mother implored me. She is afraid that out of spite he will stay home again for the whole summer this year. I see, he says, I see, and becomes quite pale and old, his cheeks are suddenly so thin, oh, that is how it is, he says. Then he goes and gets my mother. They always go to the bedroom when they have something serious to discuss.

Father tells Mother what he thinks of me, she tells me what Father said, Grandmother comes and wants to go into the bedroom, she always wants to go in when someone gets married, when someone dies, then they always discuss in the bedroom what to wear, yes, what will they wear this time? Why is it that the family never comes along to the divorce? I hear Mother sob. Now he's really given it to her. Grandmother sticks her head out the door, and you can see that she doesn't quite know where she's at. Mother is crying and can't be comforted. This is a real chance to get rid of permitted and forbidden tears. Father explains to Grandmother what has happened, and now she says, she always knew: this child should have been brought up in boarding school.

Rolf and my father still call each other by first names. They'll probably remain allied. Shall I return to our apartment with Rolf now? Shall I stay here? Where do I belong? But Rolf takes my coat and his coat. Perhaps he takes my coat because he bought it. In any case he'll have to pay back the dowry. Perhaps they talked about how they would transfer the money in monthly amounts. Grandmother hinted that she won't survive this. But the mayor says hello to us, the tobacconist still says hello to us because they don't know anything, after all I don't let them see what I'm really like, how I have destroyed everything. Why must I be like this, don't cry in the street, don't make a scene, and in the apartment the furniture is standing there as if nothing were wrong, still my kitchen, my balcony, if I want to, my, our bed, my, our floor, I may stay here if I want to, he is good to me, he knows how I am, our lampshades, our color TV, if I'll be good and agreeable, now finally I cry, Grandmother should see that, because at home she looked at my mother, passed her hand over her apron and looked at me: There, she is crying, and you?

Rolf is exhausted. I have drained him in this marriage. He lies down on that half of the bed where he has always lain because it is his half of the bed. He is lying on the left and he never asked if we should trade places even once. He doesn't see a reason, unless perhaps I was not comfortable. No, just like that. Let me lie on your half for once. Why? I want to try it. Why? He doesn't understand, takes his technical journal and has our future unfolded in front of him, if only I am reasonable and come to my senses. Isn't it insane to leave this paradise, only because this man here bores me? His hypocritical walks. He never wanted to go, but recently he has always accompanied me, just to show them all. He never felt like sitting down again with me on the worm-eaten bench behind the monastery of the Brothers of St. Mary, under the tree where a thousand years ago he made plans for the wet kiss and the whole future, he did forget all that, if only he would admit it, but each time we passed by the bench recently he would say *our bench*. Because he knew that I thought that he said it, to prove to me that he always knows what I'm thinking, and Albert will one day say *our edge of the forest*.

When he didn't yet have an academic title we still had conversations. Is there anything that every human being has, no matter who. In those days he still responded to such games: Every person has eyes. Not everybody. Fine. Every person has hair. Not everybody. There are people who don't have hair anywhere, on their whole body because they are sick! Fine. And everybody has a heart. No, there are artificial hearts now. Right? Why do you ask so much? Because I want to find something that everybody has. Something that connects us all. Makes us equal. Politically? No, in general. On a human level! Everybody, everybody has a brain. Now we have it. Brain and brain, is that the same? Certainly, with some nuances. But I ask myself sometimes whether we don't have different brains, whether we don't just imagine we see the same thing, colors for example, how does someone think who is blind to red and green? Do we all smell the same smell? I used to ask myself that too, says Rolf, and I decided to assume that we all see and smell the same thing and so forth and good night. But I often assume, Rolf, that the universe doesn't exist, neither do people, that I'm just imagining everything. That's nothing new, others before you have said that. Really? Who? I want to meet them. I hope you don't mind, he said, but I want to sleep now.

Since we've been married he always says: I have to. Something else, Rolf, yesterday I put on an important face when I was drying the dishes, I pretended to myself that I was doing something very important, and suddenly I was really important to myself, and drying the dishes seemed like the most important thing in the world to me!

When he's sleeping because he has to I snuggle up to him because I feel such fear of the nights when I will be lying by myself. I will sew a doll of cloth for myself with very long arms in which I can wrap myself. Why do I want to leave him when I admit that I need him, he would ask. Because I have to. Who says so? I do. And Karl said so too. If Karl says so it must be right. Will Karl also take care of you then? No, his opinion is that everyone should take care of themselves. Karl wrote about the paths and the journey.

I wake up Rolf to tell him: You start on your way, and it is the journey there. The others whose ways have signs and whose roads are paved call out to you that you are going astray. But you don't know the name of the place, and you know that nobody is waiting there for you, only you. Yes, in Kalksburg, Rolf yawns. Karl says I am probably an artist type. Without art? You see, Karl says there are artist types who don't create any work of art their whole lives. Well there, your Karl has said something really true! And you want to be like him? No. So you see how he fared with being free and being different? Karl says—sleep now says Rolf, I do understand everything, nevertheless I have to rest, tomorrow we are picking up my mother and taking her to the railway station. Do you remember, Rolf, the first time she went to Abbano for her rheumatism treatment? She was probably just lying in the mud when you deflowered me. Who knows, he says, if I deflowered you. You didn't bleed. You think I am lying? Since you lie to yourself like that, you must automatically lie to people with whom you live. Good night!

It was so exciting. When he asked me if I would marry him, I thought then: Life is beginning. When you receive a marriage proposal you finally belong. I did always want to belong. Even in preschool. But I never belonged. Everybody was against me. I thought: I am going to preschool, but I have to be happy so I may at least pretend to belong. All that was intensified. Especially at the university. And then I met Karl, a short time before he gave up his German studies, and he said: So often I have the feeling I don't belong anywhere. I didn't want to have anything to do with a person like that, always standing on the outside. Because Rolf loved me I belonged. But then I belonged to the lemon-yellow dress. And to Albert. I wake up Rolf to tell him what Karl told me about responsibility. That you have to be responsible for yourself. Rolf takes the blanket and moves to the living room. Or did Albert say that? It is getting light outside.

I asked Rolf if I might leave him and then come back. No.

Why not? Because he's not a toy. And I asked so much that he said: All I need is for you to ask if I believe in an eternal life and the remission of our sins. Do you believe in it, I asked, but then he felt teased. You have to swallow a lot, he said, when technology didn't interest him anymore. I admired that, although he suffered from gastritis and I didn't. I believe, Rolf, that I've always admired the wrong things. How do you suddenly know what is wrong? Don't you always say that you can't make up your mind because everything is wrong and right at the same time? But I believe that swallowing everything is wrong. And since you're always swallowing, perhaps your profession is also wrong. What has that to do with my profession? Because you don't know where the whole machine you are a little wheel in is going. But you don't know either, says Rolf, what you affect with your daily actions, glances, omissions. Yes, and that distresses me!

It doesn't distress him anymore, and he wants to make it legal. On a piece of paper the judge calls me the defendant. Rolf is called the plaintiff. A no-fault divorce would have meant that Rolf, who always knows what he does and what consequences it will have, did not know at the time of contracting the marriage what he was doing. So I take the blame upon myself. Do I have anything to plead. No, I admit everything. The judge has a scar across his forehead. It glows while he is looking at me. What does he want to hear? Pornography? Probably divorces get boring after a while. Spicy stories you can tell later in the cafeteria of the courthouse are desirable. Whether I actually had intercourse with that person of the opposite sex to whom I am not married. Yes. How often? Once will suffice, I think. But it's not as easy as that. Because if Rolf later also has had intercourse with a person of the opposite sex then my one-time adultery won't count anymore. And there is no blame. Then we won't be divorced. So I had sexual intercourse several times. Why? You naughty child, tell me more precisely, don't you see that I have to know everything to be able to divorce you properly? While I admit everything, I don't tell any details. Besides, I didn't count and don't keep a log of it because I am sloppy, my husband will confirm that.

Rolf is very pale. Matured. Like on our wedding day. Do tell him to leave me alone! But Rolf always keeps his composure in front of strangers. Later he'll tell the story of his marriage in different versions. Always what the respective woman happens to want to hear. Until he finds the right one. The one who likes to hear best what he likes to tell best.

So I did sleep with Albert as often as I wanted. That is, as often as he could. Had the time, I mean. Defendant is getting insolent. The scar is shining. The defendant was obviously not ready for marriage and thus not for a decent divorce either. Section forty-seven says that one spouse can request the divorce when the other has committed adultery. Section two says that this spouse has no right to a divorce if he agreed to the adultery or purposefully made it possible or easy by his behavior. Section fifty-two says that a spouse can request a divorce if the other suffers from a serious infectious or repulsive disease when its cure cannot be anticipated in the foreseeable future. Nice sections those are! Rolf and the judge exchange glances: Defendant is ridiculing the matter. The judge wants to know if Rolf demanded indecent things of me in bed so that I would then have refused to have intercourse with him as it says in the plaint. Yes, once in a fit of anger he demanded what otherwise he only wanted in a fit of love.

What did he demand? Rolf makes a face as if he couldn't remember. What did he demand? The judge is getting curious, but it is none of his business. The judge dictates his scanty yield to the girl who is sitting behind the typewriter. None of the men can type. And are proud of it. The book is slammed shut. It's over. The judge glides out. He has dressed up as a judge especially for us. Outside, the next couple is already waiting.

How many car rides together. How often did he put his hand on my knee and I my hand on his neck. You could read the duration of this marriage in kilometers. He bought the car shortly before our honeymoon. The engine runs well because it knows that I will never again sit at the steering wheel. Never again will I lay hands on the car. Never again hands on Rolf's neck. He has just taken my hand off, carefully, with fingers wide apart. Definitively. My hands in my lap. What do I do now? I sit like a lady. Although now once again I won't belong. His hands on the steering wheel. Where Rolf has his hands everything goes together. Turning on the signal, shifting into gear, turning on the windshield wiper, turning on the windshield washer, and he thinks that at the next gas station he will have them refill the water. He used to articulate such thoughts aloud. I often got assignments when Rolf had something else to do at the gas station. Was allowed to say: Fill it up. Super. Also sometimes: Please check the oil. But I was always afraid the attendant would refuse to take orders from a parrot. Nevertheless, he showed me the dipstick and I nodded. I always nodded. I would like to put my hand on Rolf's neck because I am grateful that he is letting me ride in his car. When we left the courthouse in Linz I thought: now he'll drive me to the bus station. He's driving more slowly than usual. Probably because he is always considerate with riders who are strangers. He isn't cursing because now he doesn't want to impose his curses on me anymore. Who will iron his shirt collar? He is looking for something in the glove compartment by himself, skillfully. So he can actually do it: puts on the fingerless gloves without asking me to hold on to the steering wheel for a moment. That is all over now. He is single now. He'll marry someone who'll say: three kilometers to go, then we'll take the turn-off to Brescia. She'll be able to read road maps. He'll find a wife who has the same interests. One to whom you don't have to explain a penalty kick. Penalty? Reward? A penalty, Rolf said. But it's both, depending on which team you are for. Corner, Out, final whistle. What's a victory by points? Does it hurt the boxer? His next wife will know all that. She'll make his ideas her own and ennoble everything. She'll manage the budget so tightly that one day it will get on his nerves. That I wish for him, despite love. For I love him again since we've been divorced. I want him to stop and kiss me, that we do it here in the car, because I love him, and I want to caress his poor back because I love him because I don't have to anymore, because it wasn't him I hated but what they made of him, those people who suffered from my lemon-yellow dress, but Rolf used to spit in the holy water and was sometimes bad in school, that one I really love, the one who kissed me so sopping wet, because it was his first kiss too, I want to find him again, the one he buried, that Rolf, but he's hidden him so well. My mother also hides some things so well that she can't find them afterwards, and then she simply says she lost them.

Rolf's mother will move in with Rolf because there is much to clean and keep in order. She took my books from the shelves, separated my cooking utensils from the cooking utensils she herself gave her son for his marriage, she has also separated the kitchen towels my mother bought for me from the kitchen towels she bought. In the bedroom the curtains that Mother gave us before Rolf's mother had a chance are gone, the others are hanging there now. Why is she so angry at me? Rolf says, because his mother loves him and can't bear it when her son is wronged. I am now visiting with my parents. They lent me my old room, and in a few weeks I'll have a job. Something feminine, yet something that my parents don't have to be ashamed of. Grandmother is crying because she sees Rolf standing behind the glass door. He doesn't know if he should still address her in the familiar way. She doesn't know either. He brings a little package and apologizes that he hasn't brought it before today. It only now turned up at the cleaners. What is it? Your nightgown. I don't want my nightgown back. No cleaner works so well that I would be able to wear that gown ever again. Going, going, going, who wants the nightgown. He is holding it in his hand like a piece of dead skin.

Our child, Mother wrote on the photo album. On the first photograph a laughing baby, underneath my christened name with exclamation mark. And a laughing little girl, I remember a voice that promised me: If you laugh you get an ice cream cone. I don't remember the ice cream. Perhaps it was just a trick. The sun is blinding me as I sit in the water tub, and I am cold because clouds keep flying between the sun and the balcony. Mother writes that the tub is something wonderful in June. A bundle of low hanging diapers, there is a child in it, and Mother wrote that this surprise was particularly successful with Papa. Then the girl begins to look like me. Blessed candle, white purse, white dress. First communion. I still remember how unpleasantly the wafers would stick to the gums. You weren't allowed to chew them, after all sweet Jesus was in them, so I carefully rolled them off with my tongue. I also hadn't confessed everything and my soul was black, I was the only child in first communion who hadn't confessed everything. I was afraid of God while all the other children loved him. Mother was ashamed when I cried in the baby buggy. I wasn't able to pronounce the word boredom yet because I didn't know it, and she didn't understand that I was bored by sitting in the baby buggy. They painted my face with egg yolk and stuck knitting needles with wooden balls into my new hairdo. How much fun this children's party was, Mother writes in the album. This picture will be in the newspaper tomorrow, said Father, and I quickly stood next to him, feet together, hold still next to Father, excited and embarrassed by so much good fortune. With Father, and in the newspaper! But he just wanted me to let them take my picture without a fuss, and the picture is in the album. It was all a trick.

Brigitte Schwaiger classifies *Why Is There Salt in the Sea?* as an inner monologue rather than a novel.[1] Its dialogues and monologues create a series of images that could serve as a basis for a screenplay. In fact, this book was her first work of fiction after she had written several theater and radio plays. Although she really considers her strength to be in screenplays, she has never worked for TV or film because she has never been offered the freedom to develop her ideas in her own way. When *Why Is There Salt in the Sea?* was published in 1977 it immediately became a best seller and was quickly translated into several languages. In general her work has been more successful outside Austria than in her home country. The excessive media attention surrounding the publication of this book caused her to withdraw from the public eye for several years. To her, there was something perverse in making a star of a writer, whereas the idea of becoming a star as an actress had been very attractive to her when she was younger.

Schwaiger was born in 1949 in Freistadt, Austria, the daughter of a doctor. After her secondary education she did not study any particular subject seriously. While

1. Much of this afterword is based on my correspondence with Brigitte Schwaiger.

spending some weeks in Spain at the age of eighteen she met her future husband, a veterinarian and "Franco fascist." Married at twenty, she divorced two years later after a very unhappy marriage. In 1974 she moved to Vienna, her present residence. *Why Is There Salt in the Sea?*, which the author originally called *Situation in Prose* and the publisher retitled, does not depict Schwaiger's own husband, as has often been hinted. Instead, the book is a rather freely invented story. Schwaiger first started playing around with it in the form of an imaginary dialogue between two characters: Albert and the narrator, whose former husband is mentioned only briefly. In the final version, the narrator's inner monologue is in response to Albert's failure to understand the divorce of this couple who had seemed, to the outside world, so perfectly matched. This subject matter may be among the reasons why Brigitte Schwaiger mentions Flaubert's *Madame Bovary,* Fontane's *Effi Briest,* and Sylvia Plath's *The Bell Jar* as influences on her writing. She claims discipleship first and foremost to Gabriele Wohmann, one of the most widely read and critically acclaimed contemporary writers in Germany.

In 1978 Brigitte Schwaiger published a collection of short stories, *Mein spanisches Dorf (My Spanish Village)*, one of which takes the form of a letter from the Rolf-figure of her novel to the publisher, attempting to justify his side of the story. It is a superb sample of the author's satirical talent. Her book *Lange Abwesenheit (Long Absence)*, published in 1980, tries to come to terms with an emotionally problematic father-daughter relationship and, to some extent, the institution of the family. It starts with the epigraph: "My father's forehead, a field of ice with a tiny figure running on it. That's me and I run and run, but his head is turning. I can't get ahead this way." Schwaiger's fascination with contrasting personalities found new expression in a different sort of publication the same year. *Malstunde* (*Painting Lesson*) is a conversation with the artist Arnulf Rainer, who is co-author of the book. It was a natural outgrowth of Schwaiger's own deep involvement with art. She seriously studied painting and sculpture for a few years.

Her most recent books are Schwaiger's own favorites so far. One of them is *Die Galizianein* (*The Galician Woman*) which came out in 1982. Here too she has a coauthor, Eva Deutsch, a Jewish woman of simple background who talks about her life during World War II. The story itself is reminiscent of recent oral history collections, and the manner of recording it shows one way of preserving the material. Brigitte Schwaiger's other favorite book, published in 1984, *Der Himmel ist süss. Eine Beichte* (*Heaven Is Sweet: A Confession*), consists of the memories of a little girl growing up in the fifties in a small town in Austria.

Through the years, Schwaiger has also written poetry; very little of it has been published so far, although a volume of her poems is scheduled to appear soon. One of the poems was included in English translation in a special journal issue on literary images of women. Since it reflects the theme of *Why Is There Salt in the Sea?*, I quote it in conclusion:

I always
drank cold water
when I felt flushed.
I never
washed fruit before eating.
I went
swimming on a full stomach.
I sucked on
candy after brushing my teeth.
Harm
came to me only from
G-rated movies
with a long kiss
at the end
and
a happy wedding.
They are
still haunting me.
Perhaps
one day they will
kill me.

Translated by Sieglinde Lug,
Denver Quarterly,
vol. 17, no. 4 (1983): 25.
Reprinted by permission of the
Denver Quarterly.